Murder and Food Porn

A Northwest Cozy Mystery - Book 8

BY

DIANNE HARMAN

All rights reserved, including the right to reproduce this book, or portions thereof, in any form without written permission except for the use of brief quotations embodied in critical articles and reviews.

Published by: Dianne Harman

www.dianneharman.com

Interior, cover design and website by
Vivek Rajan

This is a work of fiction. Names, characters, places, and incidents either are the product of the author's imagination or are used fictitiously, and any resemblance to actual persons, living or dead, business establishments, events, or locales, is entirely coincidental.

ISBN: 978-1726036825

Copyright © 2018 Dianne Harman

All rights reserved.

CONTENTS

	Acknowledgments	i
1	Prologue	1
2	Chapter One	7
3	Chapter Two	15
4	Chapter Three	22
5	Chapter Four	29
6	Chapter Five	36
7	Chapter Six	43
8	Chapter Seven	49
9	Chapter Eight	56
10	Chapter Nine	62
11	Chapter Ten	69
12	Chapter Eleven	75
13	Chapter Twelve	80
14	Chapter Thirteen	88
15	Chapter Fourteen	96
16	Chapter Fifteen	104
17	Chapter Sixteen	111
18	Chapter Seventeen	118
19	Chapter Eighteen	127

20	Epilogue	131
21	Recipes	135
23	Surprise!	141
24	About Dianne	143

ACKNOWLEDGMENTS

This book was inspired by the mouth-watering images of food on Instagram, Pinterest, and other social media sites. It's almost impossible to eat in a restaurant without having someone take a photograph of their food. I have to admit I've been guilty of doing just that. Well, I don't post them on social media, but there certainly have been occasions when I've taken a photo, hoping I could recreate the presentation.

So, to all of you foodies out there – I'm with you. I completely understand and appreciate the appeal of a beautifully presented dish. Thanks for being the genesis of this book.

Although I normally have dogs on my covers, and yes, they are in this book, I opted to do what a food photographer does, let the dish be the focal point. I didn't think having a Doberman pinscher on the cover along with a fabulous grilled meat photo would work.

As always, a huge thanks to my team for designing covers, editing, coming up with ideas, copyediting, and generally making me look good. I so rely on each of you.

And to you, my readers, I hope you enjoy this book as much as I enjoyed writing it – and thanks for continuing to read my books.

PROLOGUE

Toni Adams glanced at her buzzing cell phone which was lying on the pale pink silk comforter on her bed and took a sharp intake of breath before accepting the call. Despite her desire to tell the caller exactly what she thought of him, her sunny nature and impeccable manners resulted in her sounding more pleasant than she actually felt right at that moment.

"Hi, Hector, what can I do for you?"

She'd lost count of how many times Hector Delgado had already called her that day. He was the janitor at her office building on Bainbridge Island, and the pretext for his call was a dripping faucet in the small shared kitchen on the floor above her food photography studio. She chewed her lip as he began to speak, not concentrating on what he was saying. Her head was spinning with all the things she still needed to do before leaving on her vacation the following day.

"I'm pretty sure you've got it all under control, Hector. I know you can handle it. I'm working from home today, like I told you earlier. Yes, I'll be here all afternoon, but thanks for keeping me updated, I appreciate it. I'll see you next week when I get back." Her grimace turned to a smile when her sister Hillary appeared in the doorway. "Um, I'll look forward to it too," Toni said, trying to end the call, but Hector kept talking. "I really have to go now, Hector. Bye." She gritted her teeth as she set the phone back down on the bed.

Hillary grinned, flipping her blond curls over one shoulder. "How's lover boy?"

Toni scowled. "That was Hector, and he's not my lover boy."

"He'd like to be, though. You're too nice to him. He's going to keep asking you out until you make it clear you're not interested."

"What more can I do?" Toni said as she got up from where she was sitting on the bed and walked over to the open doors that led onto the balcony with its sweeping view of Puget Sound. She rubbed the goosebumps on her bare arms and pushed the doors shut. It wasn't quite cold enough for a sweater, but the early fall afternoon was cooler than it had been of late. "I'm not sure what part of 'No' he doesn't understand."

"Maybe Hector's hoping you and Jace will break up, and he can be your rebound relationship," Hillary suggested. "By the way, I'm just getting ready to leave for a quick last-minute trip to Seattle. Do you need anything?"

Toni shook her head. "No, I'm good. It will take me a couple of hours to finish up some editing and then get my photo shots off to YumYum Magazine. I can't trust my assistant, Barrie, not to mess it up. She's been a nightmare recently. After that, whatever else is on my to do list and doesn't get done will just have to wait until we get back from our voyage to the glaciers." Toni's hazel-colored eyes shone as they met her sister's blue ones. "I'm so glad you're here. I'm sorry for having been so preoccupied since you arrived yesterday, but I promise I'll be all yours once we set off for Vancouver in the morning."

Hillary rolled her eyes. "You'd better be. I want to hear all about how things are heating up with you and Jace, and you can tell me about whatever it is at work that has been bothering you."

"What do you mean?" Toni reached both arms behind her head

and pulled the ends of her auburn ponytail tighter. It was a girlish style for a woman in her late thirties, but she always wore her hair tied back when working, otherwise her unruly mane got in the way and obstructed her vision.

Hillary frowned. "I knew it. You always fiddle with your hair when something's on your mind. Why don't I skip Seattle, and help you out here?"

Toni shooed her sister towards the doorway. "Absolutely not. I know you want to nose around Pike Place Market, and you'd be helping me by getting out of the way. Your vacation has already started. Will you be back in time for dinner this evening? My friend Cassie De Duco and her husband, Al, have invited us over for dinner at 7:00 p.m."

"Sure," Hillary said on her way out. "That sounds great. By the way, I'm taking your car to Seattle, so if I'm not back in time can you call Uber to take you to Cassie's, and I'll meet you there?"

"Good idea. I'll text you her number and address. Now go!" Toni paused, smiling as Hillary made her way downstairs. The rattle of keys and the click of the front door being closed signaled when Toni was alone again, and she wandered back into the bedroom.

A small suitcase was open on the floor, her clothes already neatly rolled and packed in it. Toni was a seasoned traveler. Her Food Porn Photography business took her out of the state of Washington a lot, and international trips were also becoming more regular. What had started as a hobby, taking photos of food for fun, had grown in five years to Food Porn being the go-to photography company for food magazines, newspaper features, cookbooks, and blogging sites. Despite the headaches the business side of things caused her at times, her love of snapping photos of delicious food items never faded. If her waistline had expanded as a result, Toni considered that a fair trade-off.

Kicking her shoes onto the rug, she lay against the stack of pillows on the bed and opened her laptop to start work. She had a home office downstairs that she rarely used, preferring to prop her computer on her knee while lounging on the bed, the sofa, or one of the comfy outdoor chairs on the patio at the edge of the sprawling garden.

Toni lost herself in her work as her nimble fingers moved the wireless mouse across the mousepad. Cutting, pasting, adding filters, and honing colors to an array of mouth-watering food shots came intuitively as a result of thousands of hours of practise. Every so often she would ask Alexa, the smart speaker in the corner of the room, to play a song she liked, or answer a question of importance.

"Alexa, what's the weather forecast for the next few days in British Columbia and Alaska?"

She and Hillary were planning on driving to Vancouver, spending two days sightseeing, and then taking a cruise from Vancouver, British Columbia to Anchorage, Alaska. On the return leg they would fly back to Vancouver and drive home.

When she was satisfied with everything she'd done, Toni fired the photos she'd edited off to the editor at YumYum Magazine with a quick email.

Steve, hope you love these. They're making me hungry, so it's just as well I'm heading out to dinner soon. It was great catching up at the shoot. Call me if you need anything else.

Best

T

She extended her pale freckled arms into a stretch before snapping the laptop shut. Glancing at her phone, she saw there were new text messages from her assistant, Barrie, and also from Hector, neither of whom she wished to communicate with. A serious talk with Barrie was long overdue, but she decided it could wait until after she got back from her vacation. Glancing at her watch, she jumped up. There was still no word from Hillary, but it was definitely wine o'clock.

Toni made her way downstairs to the kitchen in her bare feet, walking across the stone tiles to the giant steel refrigerator. Not for the first time, she marveled to herself how she had ended up in this amazing home, which was far too big for one person, and literally straight from the pages of a magazine. She'd snapped it up as a pocket listing when it was featured in a Bainbridge Island Homes supplement for The Seattle Times. One of the home stagers who'd worked on it had tipped her off that the owners would accept an offer. She hoped one day to have a family to fill the empty rooms with noise and laughter.

Jace and I will have beautiful babies, she thought as she smiled to herself, thinking of their dinner date the evening before. Jace had made his feelings for her very clear, and for Toni, Jace was "The One." Just thinking about him gave her a warm and fuzzy feeling. She'd been married before, when she was just out of college, but it hadn't lasted. They were both too young, but they'd gone ahead with it against everyone's better advice.

"When you're twenty-three you think you know it all," her mother had warned her. "Don't blame me when it all ends in tears."

It did, and she didn't.

Toni returned the warning when her mom, Sheila, had remarried several years after Toni's dad had died.

"When you're sixty-three you think you know it all," Toni had said while fixing Sheila's veil, because Sheila had insisted on another church wedding for her second-time-around. "I hope it works out for you, Mom, I really do."

There was no getting through to Sheila that her boy toy, Ethan, was only after her for her money. It was way too late for that by the time the wedding march had started up and Toni was walking her mother down the aisle before giving her away, to a husband who wasn't much older than Toni.

She poured a glass of wine from one of the several bottles in the wine fridge, and made her way into the great room, getting no satisfaction from the memory of her mother's ill-fated marriage and having been proven right. The money had lasted just about as long as her mother, who had died at sixty-eight. The death certificate may have said the cause of death was heart failure, but Toni knew it was a broken heart.

The sound of footsteps in the kitchen caused her to turn. "Hillary? I'm in here." A look of surprise crossed her face when she saw who was coming through the doorway. "Oh, it's you."

Her killer was holding a gun and rapidly walked towards her.

"Maybe we can talk about this," Toni said in a frightened voice, while she stepped backwards until she felt the mantel behind her. The cold steel muzzle of the gun was pushed against the skin on her neck.

Her killer smiled. "I don't think so. It's a bit late for that."

The gun cracked twice. Toni's wine glass hit the floor first, the liquid seeping into the carpet. A split-second later Toni's body fell to the floor in a pool of white wine mixed with blood.

CHAPTER ONE

"Somethin' smells darn good," Al De Duco said as he walked into the kitchen of his Bainbridge Island home, followed by his majestic Doberman, Red. "What'cha makin' us fer dinner?"

His wife Cassie, who was chopping onions on a wooden board for their salad, looked up. "Out," she ordered when she saw the two of them, raising her arm and pointing the knife towards the doors that opened onto the patio. "How many times have I told you not to come into the house when you're dripping wet? If you insist on going swimming in your clothes, you could at least take off your soggy things before you come inside."

Al smirked. "Don't think Dino Arygros would appreciate it. He waved at me from his garden while we were comin' in."

Cassie lowered the knife and resumed chopping. Al and their neighbour Dino were regular sailing companions and had become good friends. The fact that their gardens bordered on the shores of Puget Sound meant they were ideally placed to jump into Al and Cassie's sailboat or Dino's cigarette boat any time the two men decided they needed to be out on the Sound.

Which was often.

"Hmph. I'm sure it would take more than the sight of you in your underwear to scare Dino," Cassie said with a bemused frown. "What happened anyway? Did you fall into the Sound again?"

Al chuckled. "Not me, it was Red, messin' around like he does all the time when he sees some of them ducks in the water. He went over the side, and I threw him the life ring. I jes' jumped in the drink to keep him company."

Cassie raised her eyes. "Somehow, I doubt it was Red fooling around. I don't think he has much of a sense of humor, unlike Balto. He's the straightest dog I've ever met." Red stared at Cassie then wandered outside, leaving a trail of water behind him.

Cassie's face turned into a scowl at the sight of the puddles on the floor.

Al took that as his cue to leave. "Pass me a cold one, will ya' Cassie? Ima gonna' get outta yer' way and hit the patio. It's a nice evenin'. I can dry off in the late sunshine."

"I'll bring one out," Cassie said with a half-smile. "Along with a towel and some dry clothes."

A few minutes later, Cassie joined Al on the patio, where he was sprawled out on a chaise lounge, his wet clothes piled in a discarded heap on the ground. "Here," she said, throwing him a towel and some shorts. "Try and maintain some modesty." She disappeared back inside and returned with a bottle of beer along with a glass of wine for herself. "I hope you haven't forgotten we have company coming for dinner, so you still have to shower."

Al pulled on his shorts and Cassie handed him his beer. He joined her at the table overlooking the garden, where Red was looking for a squirrel in the thick undergrowth under the shady tall pine trees that ringed the perimeter of the garden.

Al took a swig of his beer and lazed back in his chair. "Man, this is the life. What'd ya' say was fer dinner, and who's joinin' us?"

"I'm cooking gourmet patty melts along with barbecued peaches. The patty melt was served at a restaurant I reviewed recently, and I persuaded the chef to give me his top-secret recipe." Cassie smiled, sipping her wine. "It's one of the perks of being a food critic for The Seattle Times, I guess."

"Yeah, yer' a cheap date these days," Al said with a twinkle in his eye. "I'd kinda' like to take ya' somewhere fancy where I get to pay for a change, instead of the check bein' comped every time we go to eat. Why don't we both get all gussied up and do that tomorrow night?"

Cassie's face lit up. "You've got yourself a date, handsome."

"Great." Al leaned over and placed a gentle kiss on Cassie's lips. "Yer' pretty cute yerself. Tell ya' what, whaddya' say ya' go to the salon beforehand while I'm at work, get yer' nails painted or yer' hair curled or whatever goes on in them places." He grinned. "My treat."

"Sure, Al," Cassie said smoothly. "What's yours is mine, and what's mine is mine, right?"

Al chuckled. "That's about right. No wife of mine puts her hand in her wallet with Al around." He gazed at her with adoration, his voice cracking. "There ain't nothin' pleases me more than makin' ya' happy. Did I ever tell ya' how lucky ya' are?"

"All the time, honey, all the time," Cassie said, and she grabbed Al's hand and squeezed it tightly. It was hard to believe that just a year earlier she had been married to someone else, before her life was upended when her former husband, Johnny Roberts, was murdered on a golf course in Whistler, British Columbia.

Meeting Al had been unexpected, but they'd fallen head over heels for each other, and Cassie had grabbed the opportunity for a second shot at happiness in a heartbeat when Al had proposed. "But I already tell myself that every day."

Al gently wiped her cheek. "Now don't ya' go and start cryin', sweetheart. Not even with them happy tears. What time are our guests coming fer dinner?"

"Toni should be here about 7:00 p.m. Hillary might be a little later." Cassie checked her watch. "We should probably think about getting ready soon. Dinner's all taken care of except for you doing a quick barbecue." She glanced back at Al, who was looking confused.

"Tony Macaroni is coming here for dinner? Over my dead body. Or his, if he dares show up."

Cassie sighed. "No, it's my friend Toni Adams, silly, not Tony from the sailing club. I'm sure his name's not Macaroni, by the way. Don't you mean Marconi?"

"Tony fulla' baloney, if ya' ask me," Al said with a shrug. "Can't stand the guy. Yer' Toni, on the other hand, is a lot of fun to be around. She's the photographer who makes food look sexy, right?"

"That's the one."

"Who's Hillary?"

"Toni's sister, she's visiting from the Florida Keys. That's where they're both from. She's a real estate agent, I think."

Al's eyes lit up. "That's interestin'. Ima gonna' have to talk to her about keepin' a lookout fer an investment property fer us. Did I ever tell ya' how me n' Vinny talked about movin' to Florida one time, 'cuz there's no personal income tax there? Then we decided it was safer to just put our money in the Caymans instead." He winked at Cassie.

Cassie, well used to Al's stories about his time in the Mob with his now deceased boss, Vinny, was happy to humor him. "Speaking of Vinny, I just remembered I have some lovely news for you. Vinny's nephew, Clark, and Clark's wife, Roz, have just welcomed their baby twins into the world. They're calling the little boy Vinny, and the girl is Emilia, in honor of Roz's mother."

When Al heard the news, he was overcome with emotion. He set his beer bottle down on the table and buried his head in his hands. Cassie reached over and stroked his back until he composed himself. He looked up at the sky with shiny, wet eyes. "Hope ya' heard that up there, Boss." Turning to Cassie, he whispered, "That's the best news. Baby Vinny, huh? Ima gonna' teach that little guy everythin' I know. Vinny woulda' wanted me to."

"That might not be such a good idea, sweetheart. Some things are best left in the past, if you know what I mean. The type of business you and Vinny engaged in is not something a young child needs to learn, or for that matter, to even know about. But if he learns just a fraction of your honor, loyalty, and capacity for love, he'll do just fine in life."

Al looked up at the sky again. "Sorry, Boss, but Cassie's right as usual. Ima gonna' teach him the good stuff, not the bad. And little Em, too. Ya' can count on it." He turned back to his wife. "Did DeeDee call with the news? I've not spoken to Jake for a few days. It's been quiet on the work front lately, not that Ima complainin'."

"Yes," Cassie said. It was through her friend DeeDee Rogers, Roz's sister, that she'd met Al. When DeeDee and her husband Jake left for Connecticut for a while to help a friend in need, Al had stepped in to look after Jake's private investigation business while they were gone. "I'm not sure when they'll be moving back to Bainbridge Island for good, but they'll be here for a visit as soon as they can. The fact that Roz went a week over her due date has made DeeDee even more impatient to get here to see her niece and nephew."

"Me too. Ima gonna' call Clark in the mornin' to congratulate them." He slapped a bug on his leg with a loud smack and flicked the black smudge off his hairy skin with his thumb and forefinger. "That'll teach that nasty little critter to land on Al. Hope his pals were watchin'."

Cassie rose, lifting Al's beer bottle and her empty wine glass. "Time to get ready. No more beer until you're dressed."

Al got up to go inside, muttering under his breath. Cassie followed him into the kitchen, content with their version of domestic bliss.

*****

Al drummed his thigh with his fingers and Cassie gave him a warning stare.

"What's that look for? I never said nothin'," Al said sheepishly. His stomach made a loud rumbling sound and Red, who was standing by the window, turned and growled in his direction.

"Maybe not, but I know what you're thinking. And we're not starting dinner until they get here." Cassie checked her watch again. "It's not like Toni to be late and not call. I'll try her again."

Just as Cassie lifted her phone, she heard the sound of a car pulling up in the driveway. She gave Al a triumphant smile. "See, that'll be her now. I'll get the door."

Cassie returned accompanied by a pretty, bouncy-haired blond with blue eyes. Al, who had met Toni a couple of times before, stepped forward. "You must by Hillary," he said, extending his hand, "'cuz you sure as heck ain't Toni. I'm Al. Pleased to meet ya'."

"You too, Al," Hillary said, returning his handshake with a polite smile before turning to Cassie. "I'm a little worried about Toni. We agreed I'd meet her here since I borrowed her car, and she said she'd call Uber. I tried calling her to tell her I was on the way, but she didn't answer her phone."

Cassie's face clouded over. "I tried to reach her several times as well. I hope she's not sick or fallen somewhere, and she can't get to a telephone. Maybe we should go over to her place and check."

Hillary shook her head. "No, you guys stay put, and I'll go. You've been inconvenienced enough already. I'm sure it's some sort of mix-up. It's only a couple of miles, so I'll be there in no time."

Cassie looked doubtful. "If you're sure…"

Al rubbed his stomach, and Cassie glared at him. "Come right back, and we'll have dinner when you both get here," she said, walking Hillary to the front door.

Hillary began to protest, and Cassie silenced her with a pat on the shoulder. "I insist. It's nothing that won't keep, and we're looking forward to getting to know you over dinner. We'll see you in a little while."

After Hillary had left, Al sank into the sofa. "Ima gonna' eat my shoe if they don't hurry up." He stared at Red, who came across the room and began to sniff around Al's feet. "No Red, Ima kiddin'," he said, pushing him away.

Cassie came in and handed Al a bowl of chips. "Here, chow down on these. There's no need for drama. Hillary will easily be there and back with Toni in fifteen minutes, and then we can eat." She sat down beside Al and grabbed a handful of chips.

It was less than fifteen minutes later when Cassie's phone lit up and Toni's name flashed on the screen. Cassie smiled and accepted the call.

"Hello, Toni, I…"

Al watched as the expression on Cassie's face as it turned from happiness to pain. He slowly set down the almost empty bowl of chips. The sound of hysterical screaming on the other end of the line could probably be heard by Dino Argyros all the way next door.

He jumped up and told Red to heel. He didn't need to wait for Cassie to end the call to know that something terrible had happened.

"We'll be right there, Hillary," he heard Cassie say as he scrambled to find his car keys.

"Well?" he asked when he rushed back into the room with his car keys in his hand. Seeing Cassie tremble, he reached out for her, but she was already racing past him into the kitchen. When he caught up with her, she was on her knees turning off the oven, tears coursing down her cheeks.

He crouched down beside her and held her in his arms.

"It's Toni," Cassie sobbed into his shoulder. "Hillary just found her body. She's been murdered."

Al eased her to her feet. "C'mon, let's go."

CHAPTER THREE

Ethan Doyle smiled across the table at his elderly dinner companion and flashed her his megawatt smile. His dental work had been one of many extravagant gifts from his wife before she had died, but the dimple in his chin was natural and added to his charm.

"We should celebrate," he said, motioning to the waiter. "Meeting you has brought a new and beautiful light into my life, Trixie. I'm so looking forward to getting to know you a whole lot better. But there's no hurry, we have all the time in the world."

He smoothly placed his hand over hers as the waiter approached. After ordering the most expensive bottle of champagne on the menu, he leaned closer to Trixie Rothschild and laced his fingers through hers. The gaudy diamond jewelry adorning her scaly fingers hadn't gone unnoticed by him, and he estimated she had six-figures worth of rings on one hand alone. And the Cartier bracelet…dollar signs were flashing before his eyes.

"How about if tomorrow we go shopping?" He could see Trixie was enjoying the attention he was lavishing on her, and she looked at him with an adoring gaze as he spoke. "I'd like to buy you a little gift, a trinket, to show you how much you've come to mean to me. I don't say this lightly, but I've never met anyone like you. The day you swiped right on my dating profile was the day all of my dreams and wishes came true."

It was a line he used often, with every rich woman he dated. He gagged back the bile that rose in the back of his throat every time he said it, but it never failed to have the intended effect. Sure enough, Trixie gave him a gummy smile.

"You don't need to spend all your money on me, honey. A hard-working young man like you ought to be saving for your future. You've got yourself a whole lot of years ahead of you. I've lived a good life and want for nothing. Except, maybe…someone to make me feel desirable again, if you know what I mean." She pushed out her wrinkled chest for effect.

Ethan swallowed. Trixie was older than his usual conquests, a lot older, and that was saying something. Her breasts were out of proportion to her bony frame, and she was wearing a Versace number that screamed 'look at me.' He wondered what he was getting himself into, and felt an unfamiliar pang in his chest, a mix between compassion and guilt. Trying to shake the feeling, he rationalized the situation. Trixie, he reasoned, was lonely and looking for affection. He, on the other hand, was broke and in need of financial support. *You're not a fraudster,* he thought to himself. We're both consenting adults. *It's a mutually beneficial arrangement.*

In any case, it wasn't as if he had any choice in the matter. He was broke, with no income coming in, and he needed money, fast. Ethan was used to the good life, and the condo he was renting at the exclusive Waterfront Palace development in downtown Seattle wasn't cheap. He'd rented it furnished and styled by one of the city's top interior designers, Briana Roberts. Everything in it was state-of-the-art, which inflated the price tag. Ethan had never worked a day in his life, and his preferred cover was that he was a start-up entrepreneur based at home with his laptop. Unless he was able to find a source of funds without delay, he was going to have to resort to a life of crime.

His most recent meal ticket, a small inheritance when his wife died, hadn't lasted long. He'd already spent most of her money while she was alive. At least Sheila was a nice person. He wasn't sure he could say the same about Trixie, who was staring at him with narrowed eyes.

"Is everything alright?" Trixie inquired. "It doesn't look like you're paying attention. I was just saying that maybe we could have a little fun later. See if we're compatible, that kind of thing."

Trixie wasn't wasting any time getting to the heart of the matter, he'd give her credit for that. Maybe he could move things along faster than he'd thought. She hadn't given her age on her dating profile, and she'd scolded him to never ask a lady her age when he'd raised the subject on their first meeting, in a secluded corner of The Nest bar at the Thompson Hotel. Tonight, the candlelight in the restaurant was kind to her. He had to admit she was well-preserved, but she looked way too old to be even thinking about the things that were clearly on her mind.

"I like your style, Trixie," he said, toying with his champagne glass. "What say we skip dinner, just get the check, and hightail it out of here. Your place or mine?"

He signaled to the waiter and made a show of patting his pockets for his wallet. "Oh," he said, his face falling. "This is so embarrassing. My wallet must be in the car. I wonder…"

"If I'd cover it?" Trixie batted her eyelashes. "Without seeing what else you have to offer me in the pleasure department? I don't think so, not until I know if you've got what it takes to keep me happy."

Ethan's shoulders shook as he laughed. "Oh, I've got what it takes alright, don't you worry about that, darling." He nodded at the waiter, who had set the check on the table, and stood up. "I just remembered, my wallet's not in my car, it's in my coat. Don't go anywhere, I'll be right back." He leaned down and brushed his lips against Trixie's before sauntering towards the cloakroom without a backwards glance.

Once past the bar and out of sight of Trixie, his pace quickened. He checked out his coat, tipped the assistant with a handful of nickels and dimes, and hurried out of the restaurant. Paying the check for the meal was not an option. He knew exactly how much was in his bank account, and it wouldn't have covered a bowl of olives at the bar, never mind the champagne.

His car, a beat-up old Chevrolet, was nothing to write home about either. It was in the underground parking space that was included with his apartment rental, almost out of gas. He walked the short distance from the restaurant to the Waterfront Palace, looking over his shoulder as he went to make sure Trixie hadn't sent someone from the restaurant after him. At least she didn't know where he lived, not that he thought she would try to contact him again. Trixie was just as mercenary as he was, in her own way.

In his condo, he poured himself a scotch and wondered how it had come to this. He'd never intended to become a kept man, it had just kind of happened. He'd met his first sugar momma when he was in college. The rich, bored housewife mother of one of his friends had made her intentions very clear when he'd visited their home while he was on summer vacation before his senior year. Once he got the taste for the perks that came with being a wealthy woman's plaything, he saw no reason to change his ways. It was an easy rut to get into.

The only woman he'd ever met who had made him question his lifestyle was Toni Adams. Bubbly, funny, beautiful Toni. He'd already been dating her mother Sheila for a while before he met her two daughters, Toni and Hillary. Hillary was arguably the prettier of the two, but it was Toni who stole his heart. He'd tried everything to get close to her, but she wouldn't have anything to do with him. He'd even moved to Seattle after Sheila died to try and get Toni to give him a chance, but that hadn't helped. She still didn't want anything to do with him.

He decided he had nothing to lose. He reached for his phone and pressed her number.

She answered after one ring and yelled into the phone, "I thought I'd told you to stop calling me."

Ethan closed his eyes and smiled. The sound of her voice made him happy.

"Tell me, Ethan Doyle, are you still scouring obituaries in the newspaper and gate-crashing funeral parlors so you can befriend little old ladies whose husbands have just died? Or pretending to be something you're not on the Rich & Not Famous dating app? I don't know how you can look at yourself in the mirror without throwing up."

Ethan sighed. "Toni, I didn't call to argue with you. I'm begging you to just give me a chance. One hour, is all, to let me explain. I moved to Seattle to be close to you. Doesn't that mean anything to you?"

"It means you're stalking me, that's what it means. What kind of a man buries his wife then moves across the country to try and woo her daughter? A very sick, twisted excuse for a man, that's who."

"I knew it. I think you feel something for me, but you won't admit it to yourself."

"Oh, I feel something for you alright. Not hatred, because I refuse to be consumed by anything that would waste my time even thinking about you. That would be like me drinking poison and hoping you would die. No, my feeling for you is more like pity for your sad existence and worry for your next victim. But that person sure won't be me."

Toni's tone stung Ethan no less than if she had slapped him on the cheek. He refused to back down. Besides being his dream woman, and feisty as well, Toni had money. It was win-win, for him at least. He was sure if he could just get her into bed she'd change her mind. Many notches on his bedpost had made him an accomplished lover, and it was where he'd sealed his future with most of his conquests. Toni's mother Sheila was an exception, having insisted on waiting until they were married to consummate their union. By then, Ethan had no incentive to perform, and the marriage was mostly celibate, although Ethan played away from home when he got the urge.

"Please, Toni, if you have any compassion at all, meet me for coffee. I promise no strings will be attached."

"Contact me again, and I'm calling the cops and filing a stalking complaint against you. Is that clear? You're a liar and a thief, and that's probably not the half of it. Stay away from me and stay away from my sister. You are not welcome in our lives, and I will do whatever it takes to discredit you at every opportunity, so remember that." Toni's voice was shaking.

Ethan wasn't sure if he liked this Toni, the one spitting venom at him on the other end of the line. "That sounds nasty, baby. What did I ever do to you to make you feel like that? I'm sure I can make it better, if you'll let me try."

"You killed my mother, Ethan, with your empty promises." Toni was screaming now. "You took every spark of life she had left and squeezed it out of her, then hung her out to dry. Maybe she wasn't rich enough for you, was that it?"

Something snapped inside Ethan. "We would have had plenty of money if she hadn't split half of it between you and your brat of a sister," he sneered. "Don't talk to me about taking your mother's money. You've got that on your own conscience as well. It's not as if you needed it either, you've got plenty of your own."

"Right, and guess how I got it? It's called work. It's spelled WORK, in case you don't know how to spell it. It's a word you're obviously not familiar with. And my conscience is clear, so don't try and pull that one on me."

Ethan gave it one last shot. "I'll do anything to make it up to you. Please, hear me out. Can I come and meet you?"

"Absolutely not." Toni sounded calmer. "Hillary's in town this week, and we're going away for a few days. We leave Thursday morning. Whatever designs you have on me, or my money, you can forget about them. It's not happening. Goodbye, Ethan. I never want to see or hear from you again."

The line went dead.

Ethan lifted his glass of scotch off the table and hurled it against a nearby wall, where it smashed into jagged shards which sprayed the room. A trickle of brown liquid stained the pristine wall.

He was done. There was nothing left to lose. Toni Adams would regret the conversation they had just had, he'd make sure of it. He couldn't wait to make her squirm. She would be seeing him again, and it would be sooner rather than later.

CHAPTER THREE

Al drove at breakneck speed to Toni's house, Cassie making no attempt to urge him to slow down. They didn't pass many cars along the route to their destination, which was on the road to the Country Club of Seattle, towards the south end of the island. Al screeched the car to a halt just inches from where Hillary was standing out front, wringing her hands. The car stopped so close to Hillary she had to jump out of the way, afraid she'd be run over.

Cassie hurried out of the car and ran to Hillary with open arms, soothing the young woman she'd only met for the first time that evening. Al pulled a gun from his waistband and whispered a command to Red, who immediately disappeared into the bushes that lined the driveway, while Al waited alongside Hillary and Cassie, where he scrutinized the house.

Toni's was an old gate lodge that had been transported to the shores of Blakely Harbor. The timeless brick exterior looked as though it had been recently lovingly restored, and an array of beveled glass French doors were visible along one side, leading into the house from the waterfront patio. Up two steps and through the open front door into the hallway he could make out hardwood floors, silk-paneled walls, and a narrow staircase leading up to what he supposed was a converted loft. The original building would not have had an upstairs.

Al caught Cassie's eye, and made a hand signal gesture towards the door. Cassie pulled away from Hillary, who was still clinging to her, and Al approached the two women.

"Hillary, Ima gonna' go inside, okay?"

The young woman nodded, sniffing, and Al produced a clean handkerchief from his pocket and handed it to her. Her eyes were red and puffy, her cheeks marred by angry pink blotches.

"Can you tell me where Ima gonna' find Toni?" Al's voice was gentle.

Hillary involuntary shuddered. "In the great room. It's through the hallway and to the right of the kitchen." She looked from Al to Cassie and then back to Al. "I can't go back in there. Please, don't make me."

"You don't have to do anything," Cassie said, placing an arm around her shoulder. She looked for somewhere to sit. Hillary was shivering. "Why don't we wait on the front steps over there," Cassie said, "or we could sit in the car if you're cold?"

Hillary moved towards the steps, where she huddled next to Cassie while blowing her nose into the handkerchief.

Al whistled for Red, who had made his way through the bushes into the garden and now reappeared from the opposite side of the house. Red entered the house first, followed by Al, who had his gun at the ready in his hand. They walked along the hallway where family photos adorned the walls. A laughing Toni beamed out from a beach shot where she was standing with Hillary and a smiling older woman who Al assumed was their mother.

Red growled as they neared the back of the house.

"Stay," Al commanded Red, and he walked past the kitchen to the doorway of the great room. Red growled louder. "On guard." The big dog was obviously disturbed about something in the great room.

The door was ajar, and Al pushed it open with his shirt-sleeved elbow. The room was luxurious, decorated in a traditional style that complemented the historical period of the house. Several food magazines were strewn across a coffee table, and on the wall was a framed YumYum magazine cover with a colorful picture of a fruit salad platter. Al had seen it before, when Cassie bought the magazine and brought it home after Toni's firm had won an award for the cover. Cassie had explained to him the fruit was, in fact, laid out on a naked woman's torso.

"Eww. Don't be gettin' any ideas," Al had said when she showed it to him. "I like eatin' my strawberries from a dessert bowl, not yer' belly button, if that's alright with you." Cassie had assured him it was.

He swept around the room with the muzzle of his gun, but he didn't see any signs of danger. A recessed bar area in the corner was fully stocked with liquor bottles and glasses for entertaining in style, but Al's eyes were drawn to the lifeless body sprawled on the carpet between the coffee table and the hearth. The auburn ponytail identified it as Toni, and Al inched forward, avoiding stepping on the blood and fragments of broken glass that were on the carpet. Checking for a pulse was a rudimentary exercise which served to confirm what he already knew. Toni was dead, He estimated she'd been that way for a couple of hours at least. Being careful not to touch anything, he and Red made their way back outside where Cassie and Hillary were waiting for them.

Cassie's gaze met his, and Al gave her a sad shake of his head. He cleared his throat. "Hillary, Ima gonna contact the police, unless you already did?"

"No, I just grabbed Toni's phone to call you when I found her and then I came outside, like Cassie suggested," Hillary said. "I must have dropped the phone after that. It wasn't in my hand when I came out, and I was too afraid to go back inside." She began to sob again.

"That's okay. I'll deal with it," Al said. He walked to the car where he dialed 911 out of earshot, so as not to cause Hillary further distress. When he was done, he placed his gun in the glove compartment, locked it, and then opened the trunk, pulling out a couple of blankets. Returning to the house where the two women were sitting on the front steps, he handed one to Cassie and draped the other one loosely around Hillary. "Try to stay warm," he said. "It might be a long wait."

Al was surprised when several police cars arrived at the property within a matter of minutes. He knew the Bainbridge Island Police Department was a small one, and the scale of the police response struck him as unusual, and that they had arrived so soon after his call. A tall man wearing a tuxedo got out of the first car and approached them.

"Chief Hewson," Al said, walking over to meet him. "What are you doing here?"

Dan Hewson, Chief of the Seattle Police Department, greeted him with a solemn handshake. "This evening is the annual police awards dinner for the Bainbridge Island Police Department, and I was on my way there to serve as the Master of Ceremonies. We work closely with the team here, as you well know."

Al nodded.

"When the dispatcher took your call, we were about to leave the precinct for the dinner, and the local chief asked who called it in. Said it was a man by the name of Al De Duco." Dan smiled at Al. "I said I knew you and would swing by to help. What happened?"

Al told him about the events of the evening, culminating with finding Toni's body at her home. He returned to Cassie while Dan took command. The sirens and the arrival of the swarm of police officers had set Hillary off again, and she was crying hysterically. A paramedic attended to her before a female officer steered her into the back of one of the patrol cars to take a statement from her.

Al placed his hand in the small of Cassie's back and she leaned into him, her head not reaching his shoulder. Red stood still beside Al while Cassie and Al were in turn interviewed by the police.

"Like I tol' ya', we ain't seen nothin'," Al confirmed to the officer who took his statement. "Jes' came straight here after Hillary called. I sent my dog sniffin' around before I went in." He motioned to the open door. "But whoever bumped Toni off is long gone, I reckon."

Chief Hewson came up at that moment and spoke to the officer. "I'll take over here, thanks, Joe." Looking around for a quiet spot, the chief took Al aside. "Tell me about the decedent, Al. Did you know her well?"

Al shook his head. "I met Toni once or twice, but Cassie knew her far better than I did. They move in the same sort of foodie circles. I don't know much about food, apart from eatin' it."

A faint smile crossed Dan's face. "I'm much the same. I'm a big fan of your wife's food columns in The Seattle Times. Mrs. Hewson and I have discovered several new restaurants through her Food Spy recommendations. In fact, Cassie was just telling me she'd been working with Toni Adams to publish a recipe book. I'm sorry that won't be happening. It would have made a lovely present for my wife."

"That's right. Cassie had chosen some of her top-rated dishes from her reviews and various chefs had volunteered the recipes. Toni was in charge of takin' pics of them. All the proceeds were goin' to the Seattle Foundation." Al sighed. "Cassie's gonna' be disappointed to let the Foundation down, but there ain't much she can do about that now, I guess. I jes' hope you guys find Toni's killer and get to the bottom of why they did this. Toni was pretty well-liked, from what I heard."

The chief frowned. "Al, I have to tell you, the Bainbridge Island Police Department is really understaffed right now. As a matter of fact, their police chief and I were just talking about it earlier. They've only got a couple of detectives and a dozen or so patrol officers. They're already stretched to the limit. Technically, this is outside my jurisdiction, but I'll see what I can do. I was thinking…" He paused, and Al waited for him to continue.

When the chief remained silent, Al spoke up. "C'mon, spit it out, Chief. Ima gettin' the feelin' there's somethin' yer' not sayin.'"

"You'd be right. Look, I know Jake is in Connecticut and that you've taken over his private investigation firm while he's gone. And you've got Luke Robertson on your team, a well-known ex-cop."

Al chuckled. "You should know, you trained him."

"Exactly. I was sorry to lose him when he left the force, but I understand his reasons. When his fiancée was murdered at Le Bijou Bistro, the police weren't able to find her killer due to lack of resources. You and Jake found the murderer, Al, not Seattle PD. Do you see where I'm going with this?"

Al looked across to where Hillary had rejoined Cassie.

"You might want to talk to Hillary and see if she'll hire you," Dan continued. "Even with the best intentions, it will probably take the force here longer to get to the bottom of this than Hillary would like. Thankfully there aren't many murders around these parts, but when it happens, they often remain unsolved for a long time. This is off-the-record, but with your, how shall I put this, background, you seem to have a knack for getting around a lot of the red tape that would delay the police in this type of investigation."

Darkness was falling, and Al adjusted the sunglasses he wore day and night. The only time he took them off was in bed.

"No idea what yer' gettin' at, but I'll take that as a compliment, Chief," he said with a nod. "Leave it with me, and Ima gonna' see what I can do. I'll let ya' know if Hillary wants to take that course of action."

Dan checked his watch and looked around. Toni's covered body was being taken out of the house on a gurney. "Looks like we're wrapping up here for tonight, but the house will be off-limits until the forensics team is finished. If Hillary wants to collect some things, she'll need to do it now before they seal the place off."

Al shook Dan's hand. "Sure. Hope ya' enjoy yer' dinner, y'all."

He watched Dan make his way over to the waiting police car and then turned to Cassie who was walking towards him.

"Hillary's still very emotional, as you can imagine," she said. "She wanted to stay at a hotel, but I told her we wouldn't hear of it. I've invited her to stay with us for a few days, if that's all right with you."

Al leaned down and kissed her. "Of course. There's plenty of room at our place. She can stay as long as she likes. Ima gonna' go inside with her, so she can pack a bag. You get in the car with Red. We'll be back in a couple of minutes."

He took a deep breath and headed for the house.

CHAPTER FOUR

Barrie Jones watched her boss, Toni Adams, spread a handful of Polaroid photographs across the conference room table. Toni's freckled hands were nimble, switching and moving the white-bordered squares around until they were placed just how she wanted.

"What do you think?" Toni asked, standing on a chair to get an aerial view of the tabletop, and nearly falling over in the process. "I know they want a time-lapse photo series of decomposing food to show how long it takes for processed food to rot, but that's way too boring. I thought if we add a small child to the photos you can see the child's development and growth in contrast to how long it takes for a processed hamburger to biodegrade."

Barrie frowned. "It's a good idea in theory, but it will be tricky to pull it off, especially when children are involved. We're talking months, right? The hamburger's not going to cause any trouble, but the kid might."

Toni laughed, as she climbed down. "You're probably right. What do you think we should do to add interest to the presentation? The client's waiting in the reception area right now, and I'd like to pitch them a couple of options. These Polaroids show the client's organic burgers alongside some equally delicious-looking but evil enemy burgers. So far, so blah." She made a face.

"I think," Barrie said, "We should give them what they want. Why make it complicated? We're getting paid to deliver photos, not come up with clever marketing concepts. You and I both know we can make the images tell whatever story the client wants." She scowled. *Why did Toni always have to overthink things?* She thought.

"Leave it to their marketing team to come up with the ideas. If they don't like your suggestions, you risk alienating them if they think you're criticizing their concept."

"Hmm." Toni thought for a moment. "I'll take that risk. I like adding creative input. Clients appreciate service providers going the extra mile, Barrie. We're all on the same side. You'll learn that as you gain more experience. It's possible to make suggestions in a way that doesn't compromise the relationship. Sometimes a client thinks they know what they want, but they really don't. If we can improve their campaign in a way that makes them think they thought of it in the first place, all the better."

Barrie nodded, getting up. "Thanks, Toni. I'll bear that in mind. I've still got so much to learn. I appreciate your patience helping me. I know I've made a few mistakes lately, and I promise it won't happen again. You can count on me."

Toni nodded, her smile fading. "I hope so, Barrie. You're a great food stylist and photographer, but if you ever send a client the wrong photos again, there will be consequences. We're lucky The Seattle Times was very understanding about it. I can't afford to lose a client of that caliber."

"I understand completely," Barrie said, dropping her head. Not because she was embarrassed by her ineptitude, but because she didn't want Toni to see the look of hatred in her eyes. "I'll go greet the clients now and bring them in," she mumbled. "Do you need anything else?"

Toni looked around the room, her eyes settling on the credenza where fresh coffee should be, but it was empty. She raised her eyebrows and stared at Barrie, who shrugged. "I didn't have time," her assistant muttered, before leaving the room.

How dare she, Barrie thought as she hurried down the hall to the reception area. *That woman's passive aggressive way of threatening me is pathetic. If she wants to fire me, she should come right out and say it. Who does she think she is, anyway? She expects me to do everything around here, including making the coffee. Ungrateful witch.*

Barrie managed to turn on a smile as she made small talk with the clients she met in the reception area and then she escorted them to the conference room where Toni was waiting.

"Thanks Barrie, that will be all for now," Toni said, making it clear her presence was not required at the meeting. "Just the coffee, when you have a minute."

When Barrie returned with the coffee, she made quite a bit of noise setting out the cups. She knew it would bug Toni, who liked quiet at all times. Pettiness was one of Barrie's strong points, and she never let go of a grudge. There were plenty of reasons why she disliked Toni, and she was done with trying to hide her feelings. Something had to change, and soon.

After excusing herself, she went outside. She stood in front of the building, taking a deep drag on her cigarette, and hoped Toni could see her from the window of the conference room upstairs. Smoking was one of Toni's pet hates, and a notice in the staff room stated smoking was to take place outside and around the side of the building, where the stinky trash dumpsters were located. Since Barrie was the only smoker on Toni's payroll, she'd taken the notice as a personal slight.

Hector, the building's janitor, approached her holding an empty bucket in one hand and a wrench in the other and said, "You'd better hope Toni doesn't see you standing there. You know she doesn't like anyone smoking out here. Not even clients, although there's not much she can say about that."

"Exactly. Why else do you think I'm doing it?" Barrie blew out a puff of smoke. "I'm sick of all of her stupid rules."

Hector raised an eyebrow. "What's got you so snarky today? I thought you two were getting along okay."

"Not so much." Toni Adams may have topped Barrie's list of least favorite people, but she wasn't about to explain herself to Hector. "Just because you're her number one fan, doesn't mean we all share your sentiments. She's never going to go out with someone like you, anyway. Beats me why you keep asking her."

Hector's face clouded over.

"What's wrong, Hector, did I touch a nerve?" Barrie let out a hollow laugh and stamped her cigarette butt into the ground with a twisting motion of her shoe.

"Make sure you pick that up," Hector said sharply. "Anyway, there's a leak in the kitchen. I'd better get going."

Barrie watched him shuffle off, his progress slowed by a limp. She leaned against the wall of the building and sighed. She despised Hector for his adoration of Toni, although Barrie and Hector were similar in many ways. They were both in their thirties, trying to make something of their lives. Like him, she'd grown up poor, however Hector mostly embraced his background and heritage, while Barrie was ashamed of hers.

She'd been raised in Tukwila, Washington, where over one-fifth of the population lived at poverty level or below. Her family was still part of the number making up that statistic, but not Barrie. Not any longer. Growing up living in Tukwila with her extended family in a mobile home park, she knew she was different from the losers in her family. She often referred to them as 'trailer trash' and couldn't wait to get out of Tukwila. She'd quit high school and moved to downtown Seattle, renting a small studio apartment in a building in a tenement district. Lacking schooling, her first job was as a house cleaner for an agency.

One of her clients, Jim, was a photographer, and he taught her how to operate a camera. The first time she saw a Canon EOS DSLR, it was love at first sight. She was a natural. Jim had become a mentor to her, and it wasn't long before he was also her lover. Through Jim's connections, Barrie secured a job as Toni's assistant, but she was tired of playing second fiddle to her boss. Barrie had much greater ambitions.

"We make a good team, don't we?" she'd whispered to Jim one night as they snuggled up on the sofa. She'd made him his favorite meal and plied him with wine. "I was wondering how you would feel about us going into business together."

Jim rubbed her back and chuckled. "I thought you didn't like being anyone's assistant. You're not great at taking orders. I wouldn't want you to turn against me if you were mine."

Barrie shook her head. "No. I don't want to be a corporate headshot photographer, and you've said yourself it's boring and underpaid. Food is where it's at. With the rise of all of the food blogs on the internet covering every type of cuisine, the best photographers can name their price. I should know. I've seen Toni's invoices and bank statements." She leaned over and kissed him.

Jim looked confused. "You mean, go into competition with Toni? I don't think so. She'd be a tough cookie to go up against."

Barrie topped off his wine glass. She'd already played out the conversation many times in her head. "You've got that money you inherited, and you've been waiting for the right business opportunity to come along. Why not make her an offer to buy her business? She'd have to agree to a non-compete clause for a certain period of time, but by then we'd be so successful it wouldn't matter if she started up again under a new name. Don't you see? With me running the business and both of us taking the photographs, we wouldn't need any other staff apart from a receptionist, which would increase the profits instantly." Her eyes shone. "Together, we would be unstoppable!"

Barrie didn't mention the part about how the plan would secure her future. Jim had made it clear from the outset of their relationship ten years earlier that he never wanted to get married or have children. The financial security of a business jointly owned by the two of them would be her little insurance policy in case they ever broke up.

Once Barrie had planted the seeds of the idea in Jim's head, she was surprised by how fast things moved. He loved the idea, and had consulted lawyers, moved funds, and even looked at business premises in Seattle. Barrie said she didn't want to have to travel to Bainbridge Island to work, and Jim agreed that a base in the city made a lot more sense.

The plan fell apart at the last hurdle, when Jim arranged a meeting with Toni to lay out his intentions and make her an offer.

"I could have saved you the trip, Jim, if you'd told me what this was about before you came all this way," Toni had said when Jim explained the reason why he'd wanted the meeting. Barrie, who happened to be in Toni's office when Jim made his ill-fated offer to buy her business, would never forget the withering look on Toni's face as she continued, "I thought you were here to see your girlfriend," she said, nodding towards Barrie. "Food Porn Photography is not for sale. Not now, and not ever."

That look said a thousand words. Barrie was pretty sure Toni had some idea about the source behind Jim's plan to buy the business. *Ever since then, she's treated me like scum,* Barrie seethed. *Toni, with her stupid ponytail and cute freckles. Always pretending to everyone that she's Miss Sweetness and Light. Why can't people see what she's really like?*

A blond head appeared around the front door of the building. Angela, the receptionist, called across to her. "Barrie, Toni's looking for you. She's not too happy. Something about the proofs for the Munchies pitch being covered in coffee stains."

Of course, it's my fault as usual, Barrie huffed, as she made her way back inside. *I'll be glad when she goes to Alaska on that stupid boat trip and gives us all a break for a few days. Maybe she'll fall off the boat and freeze to death and never come back.*

That's when it hit her. Of course! The only way to make sure Toni would never bother her again was to get rid of her once and for all. If Toni died, the business would be put up for sale, and Jim would be able to buy it as they'd planned. He'd probably even get a better price.

She smiled. It was so simple. So perfect. And there was no time to waste.

CHAPTER FIVE

Back at home, Cassie did her best to salvage the meal she'd prepared earlier.

"I don't know about you ladies, but I could do with a drink," Al announced, opening the refrigerator and taking out a beer. "Anyone care to join me?"

Cassie nodded. "Wine for me, please, and after you get drinks, would you start the barbecue?

"Hillary? Ya' joinin' us?" She nodded as well.

Hillary accepted her glass of wine with a grateful smile. "I hope the police can quickly find out who did this to Toni," Hillary said with a frown. "I'm still processing everything that's happened, but I don't think I can start to grieve or move on with my life until the killer has been caught and brought to justice. My head is spinning right now with everything I need to do. Toni's business, her house, the funeral arrangements…" Her voice trailed off. "I have no idea where to start."

Cassie gave Hillary's hand a reassuring squeeze. "Don't try to think about all of that tonight. Right now, you need to eat and then get some sleep. Al and I will help you tomorrow with whatever else needs to be done."

"Al, will you please cook these hamburgers on the barbecue and then bring them in to me when they're ready? When you're finished with the burgers, you can cook the peaches on the barbecue while I finish up these patty melts. It's a little late, but at least the food won't be stale."

A few minutes later Al took a big bite out of his patty melt and said, "This was worth the wait. Very tasty. I've had worse meals in some of them fancy restaurants."

Hillary picked at her food and moved it around on her plate with her fork, obviously not in the mood to eat anything. "Al, did the police give you any idea how long it will take to wrap this up?" Do you know if we're talking days, weeks, or longer? Obviously, I won't be going to British Columbia as planned…"

Tears welled up in Hillary's eyes, and she struggled to compose herself. "What I mean is, my work back home is taken care of until next week. But if I'm not going to be returning to Florida by then, I need to contact some people to let them know."

Al chewed slowly, remembering his conversation with Chief Hewson. He looked at Hillary and sensed a strength within her. In spite of everything that had happened, she was thinking rationally and trying to anticipate the practicalities of what lay ahead. He decided honesty was the best policy. "Ima not gonna' sugarcoat this, Hillary, but the way Chief Hewson was talkin', it's lookin' like it could be quite a while. He was tellin' me the police force here on the island is stretched to the limit right now. It ain't likely they're gonna find Toni's killer within days, maybe even weeks."

"I see." Hillary turned her wine glass around in her hands, deep in thought.

Al noticed Hillary hadn't eaten any of her food. "If yer' plannin' on stickin' around to see this through, ya' might have to cancel all of yer' appointments back home fer the foreseeable future," he added.

"There's no question of me leaving town until Toni's killer has been found. That's simply not an option." Hillary looked at Al, her eyes imploring him. "Al, would you consider taking the case on? Toni told me about your success in solving the recent murder at the Waterfront Palace. Money's no object, so if you need to employ extra help to cover the rest of your workload, I'll meet the costs, no problem."

"Lemme' ask the boss here." Al turned to Cassie. "If ya' don't mind me postponin' our date we had planned for tomorrow night, I think I can get started right away."

Cassie smiled at her husband. "Fine, but I'll hold you to it as soon as you close the case." To Hillary she added, "Between work and sailing, I hardly ever see Al these days."

"Ima keepin' her on her toes." Al winked at Hillary before his expression turned serious. "Looks like ya' hired yerself' a private investigator. I hate to do this, but there's no time to waste. Is there anythin' at all ya' can tell me about anyone who mighta' wanted to kill Toni?"

Hillary looked confused. "Not that I can think of. Her friends loved her. She was the most popular person I know, literally the life and soul of the party."

Cassie cleared the dinner plates from the table. Hillary's patty melt had gone untouched, so Cassie chopped it up into bite-size pieces and scraped it into Red's dog dish. Then she prepared three bowls of ice-cream from a tub she found in the freezer. "I hope you like Italian ice-cream," she said to Hillary as she returned to the table. "There's a fantastic place on the island, Da Vinci's. It's homemade, just not by me."

Hillary's eyes lit up, and she began to eat. Wordlessly, Cassie set the tub on the table in case their guest wanted seconds, throwing Al a warning look not to touch it.

Al had been considering what Hillary had told him and changed his line of questioning. "Okay, let's take a different angle. Can you think of a motive anyone might have had for murderin' Toni? Ima thinkin' money, revenge, things like that, ya' know whadda mean?"

Hillary looked over to where Red had gotten up from his dog bed in the corner of the kitchen and wandered over to his dog dish by the patio doors, drawn by the smell of the recently cooked patty melt. He began to eat with gusto, happy to have a little dessert after his regular meal of dry kibble.

"Yes, I understand," she said. "Toni was wealthy in her own right, in that she had a successful business. She also inherited money when our father died. As a matter of fact, we both did. Half the proceeds of his life insurance policy was split between me and Toni. The other half went to our mother."

She let out a hollow laugh. "Or rather, it went to the gold digger boy toy she married a year later. Money could have been a motive, except as far as I know, I'm Toni's only beneficiary. And I've got plenty of money of my own."

Al reached for a notebook and pen and opened the notebook to a clean page. "Yer' not a suspect yet, don'tcha worry. What's yer' mother's husband's name?"

"Ethan Doyle."

"Where does he live, this stepfather of yours?" Al asked.

Hillary shrugged. "I have no idea. After Mom died, I never saw him again. When she was ill, I made it very clear to him exactly what I thought of him. I told him he was a good-for-nothing creep. I had him checked out when Mom seemed short of money, you see. He'd always claimed he was an internet entrepreneur who invested in startups, but I couldn't find a trace of any of his companies. When I called him on it, he accused me of meddling and trying to turn Mom against him."

She paused, staring at Red, before looking back to Al. "Toni disliked Ethan as well, but since she lived so far away, she never confronted him like I did," she continued. "Toni moved across the country to Bainbridge Island after our mother's marriage, because she found the situation unbearable. She told me Ethan had contacted her recently and said Mom had asked him to take care of her. In fact, she thought she saw him one time outside her house, but I told her she was probably imagining things." Smiling, Hillary continued. "Toni could be quite dramatic. She believed in the afterlife and went to several clairvoyants to try and contact Mom after she passed away."

"I remember her telling me about that," Cassie said. "I don't think they were successful."

Hillary snorted. "Of course, they weren't. What a load of mumbo jumbo. So, when she said she thought she'd seen Ethan, I didn't think anything of it. For all I know, he's still in Florida."

"I can get that checked out easily enough," Al said, scribbling in his notebook. "I'll take care of it. Anythin' else? Anyone at work botherin' her, or a romance turned sour—was she seein' anyone?"

"Yes, she had a boyfriend," Hillary said. "As far as I know they were very happy together. I think they were starting to get very serious. His name's Jace Carson. He works in television."

"That's right, I met him once with Toni," Cassie said. "He's the executive producer of several television shows that are all food and home oriented. Toni told me they met when he called her company and had her photograph several food items for an ad. Since that time whenever food photos were needed, he always had her do them." She watched Al take notes. "Like Hillary said, they were crazy about each other."

"In that case, someone better let Jace know," Al said. "Hillary, do you want me to call him?"

She shook her head. "I'll do it in the morning." Red looked up from his dog dish and took a few steps towards the table. "Hey, handsome fella," Hillary said, holding out her hand. Red walked the rest of the way over to her, allowing himself to be stroked, before resting his head on her knee.

Al scratched his head in amazement. "That's a first, Ima gonna' tell ya'. Red's not usually the friendliest of dogs, but he's taken a shine to ya'."

"The feeling's mutual," Hillary said with a smile. She stifled a yawn. "Sorry, I think it's the wine on an empty stomach. There's something else I should mention. It's probably nothing, but…"

"Go ahead," Al said, pen poised. "Ain't no such thing as nothin' when yer' sister's been shot at point-blank range." *Ima sorry Hillary had to see what that looks like,* he thought. *Ain't a pretty sight.*

"Have you ever heard of a guy called Tyler something?" Hillary directed the question towards Cassie. "I believe he runs a food blog called Nibbles."

Cassie rolled her eyes. "Yes, Tyler Alexander? He's at every food event I go to. He's a freeloader, likes to complain a lot, and thinks he's superior to everyone else in the industry."

"That sounds about right." Hillary turned to Al. "Toni was stressed about work and mentioned that this Tyler guy had been bothering her. Apparently, she did a food photo shoot for his blog and he used the photos, but he never paid her for them. When she followed up with him, he said he hated the photos and that his blog had lost followers ever since he'd used them. Not only would he not pay what he owed her, he was threatening to sue Toni for compensation unless she agreed to an out-of-court settlement."

Al thought about what Hillary had told him. "Seems like we got a coupla' good leads already." He snapped his notebook closed. "Why don'tcha sleep on it. Ya' can let me know tomorrow if ya' can think of anythin' else. In the meantime, I'll get the rest of my team onto this first thing."

Hillary's eyes shone with gratitude, and her chin wobbled. She began to say something, but Cassie beat her to it. "Ssh, it's alright.

Let's go upstairs. I'll show you to your room."

"Goodnight," Al said, watching Red follow the women into the hallway. Relieved Cassie had intervened before Hillary started crying again, he considered having another beer.

Women and their waterworks, he thought, *could drive a man to drink.*

CHAPTER SIX

"I'm sorry sir, your card's been declined. Do you have another one you would like to use?"

Tyler Alexander scowled as the assistant at the Apple store handed him back his gold Amex card. "I'm not sure why you're called a Genius," Tyler muttered, thumbing through his wallet, "when clearly you can't even work that machine hanging around your neck." He rolled his eyes and handed him a Visa card.

The Genius did something with the card on the tiny device that looked like a phone dangling around his neck on a white lanyard, before looking up at Tyler with an apologetic smile. "I'm afraid this one's no good either. If you like, we can hold your purchase until the end of the day."

The Apple Store at the Bellevue Square shopping mall was getting busy with the lunchtime crowd, and several people waiting on the stools at the Genius Bar had turned around to stare at them. Tyler debated whether making a fuss was worth it but asking the store to call his credit card company would probably lead to further embarrassment for him.

He tried to shrug it off, hoping the heat rising on his face didn't reveal his true feelings. "There must be some kind of mix up," he chuckled. His throat was dry, and he tried to swallow, but it ended up sounding like a croak. "I just got back from Las Vegas, so I guess I've maxed it out. I'll call the bank to transfer some funds and come back this afternoon. Make sure you keep that I-Baby for me until I get back, okay, dude?"

"Of course," the Genius replied, but the store assistant's attention was already focused elsewhere. He'd turned away to speak to another customer, and Tyler stole one last glance at the special edition iPhone X the Genius was carrying. Copper-plated and encrusted with Swarovski crystals, it was the object of Tyler's girlfriend's desire. And if Harper didn't get what she wanted, she'd make his life miserable.

Tyler made his way through the mall to the nearby parking structure, willing himself to ignore the designer menswear calling to him from the windows of many of his favorite stores. When he reached his car, which was on the top level, he stared at his sleek black Audi A7 for a few moments before he opened the door. He wondered how long it would be before the leasing company came to repossess it.

His payments had bounced for the last three months and the leasing firm was running out of patience, as was his landlord, his accountant, and his lawyer. He'd had to use the last cash he had to pay the web developer company who had redesigned his food blog, Nibbles, after a midnight visit from a man wearing a hoodie and carrying a baseball bat.

"You're broke," his accountant had warned him several months earlier. "You're living the lifestyle of the rich and famous, and you're neither. Not even close. Your income is dwindling and even on a good month it doesn't cover your expenses. If things don't improve, you're headed for bankruptcy court."

Tyler hadn't wanted to believe things were that bad, and he was sure he could turn his business back into the money-making machine it had been in its glory days. At one point, Nibbles was making him so much money it was like owning his very own ATM. He'd go to bed at night and wake up the next day several thousand dollars richer.

That was the beauty of the internet. For no apparent reason, several of the posts on his blog had gone viral and generated millions of page views. With the traffic came pay-per click advertising deals, sponsored posts, and lucrative product endorsements. When he'd gotten bored with his daily work routine of uploading a foodie picture or two onto his blog and pinning them on Pinterest, he paid a college student a few bucks to do it for him instead. That left all of his time pretty much free for shopping, dating, and bragging about his perfect life on social media.

Tyler stared at the Audi's dashboard, with all its fancy gadgets and extras, before banging his head several times on the steering wheel. The horn sounded, but no one was around to hear it.

Stop this, Tyler, a voice inside his head urged him. *This isn't you. You're not a quitter.*

He sat up and looked at his reflection in the rearview mirror. Apart from the red splotch on his forehead from hitting it against the steering wheel, he looked like an attractive, successful businessman in his late twenties. His Clark Kent glasses were from Gucci. He wasn't born with the chiseled features of a male model, but a pleasing appearance, confident manner, and a way of making women laugh ensured that he rarely went home from parties alone. Nice car, nice clothes. *I might have a few money problems, but who doesn't? There must be a solution,* he thought.

Until Tyler met Harper, he'd never considered settling down. In his mind's eye he could see her as he'd left her that morning - barefoot and wearing one of his shirts that swamped her petite frame. Her cherubic curls and adorable smile belied her strong character. Harper was high maintenance and made no apologies for it. Tyler knew if he couldn't keep her in the style to which she was accustomed, she would find someone else who could. He had to fix this and fix it fast.

He pulled his phone out of his pocket and scrolled through his contact list until he found the name he was looking for. Taking a slug from the bottle of water that was sitting on the passenger seat, he pressed the green button on his phone, confident of solving his little financial issue before returning home. Facing Harper without the limited-edition iPhone X in his hand was not an option.

"Toni Adams, please," he said to the receptionist at Food Porn Photography when she answered his call. "It's Tyler Alexander. Tell her it's urgent and in her interest that we speak immediately."

"Just one moment, please," the receptionist said.

Tyler heard soft floaty music in the background as he waited. And waited. He swore under his breath as he ended the call and pressed redial.

"Apparently," he shouted into the phone when it was picked up by the same receptionist, "Ms. Adams thinks it's funny to keep me on hold for over ten minutes. I'd appreciate the courtesy of her speaking with me NOW if she knows what's good for her. Otherwise, she'll regret it."

"Just one moment, please," the receptionist said.

The same floaty music was audible once again, but this time it was only for a few seconds. A short silence followed, and Tyler could sense the frostiness on the line before Toni addressed him. Her voice was sharp. "I take it this isn't a friendly call, Tyler, as my receptionist tells me you've started throwing threats around. I've told you before, I have nothing to say to you. Now that lawyers are involved, I couldn't speak with you even if I wanted to. Goodbye…"

"Toni, wait," Tyler pleaded. "I'm sorry. It wasn't a threat, what I said came out wrong. Please, just let me have a few minutes of your time to talk this through, and I'm sure we can reach an amicable agreement. I never wanted to call the lawyers in, but you left me with no choice." *And a $50,000 legal bill I can't pay,* he thought.

"Hmm. You have a unique way of twisting things around. Tyler, I'll give you that. As I recall, you never settled the account for the two day shoot I did for your Nibbles blog. Next thing I know, you're suing me?" Her voice cracked. "I'm still trying to get my head around how you want me to pay you a million dollars when you're the one who owes me. It was a measly ten grand, Tyler, and now my lawyers' fees have dwarfed that. Like I told you before, you're the last person I want to speak to. Please stop these harassing calls, or I will report you to the police for stalking me."

"Who's making threats now, huh?" Tyler said, trying to buy enough time to get his point across. "You ruined my business, Toni, with those pathetic shots of a picnic on the beach at Bainbridge Island. No one clicked on the Pinterest graphics, they were a complete disaster. And my regular blog traffic tanked right after I ran the Perfect Picnic series of articles with your images in them. I've lost all my advertisers and sponsors as a result. One year's income. One million dollars. In my lawyer's opinion, you're getting off lightly."

Toni sighed. "You know, your nose must be very long right now, just like Pinocchio's was. I'm guessing your lawyer said you don't have a leg to stand on. My photography business has no liability in connection with those photos. That's covered in a clause in our Standard Terms of Business Contract, which I assume you read before signing it."

Tyler was glad Toni couldn't see his face. What she said was true, apart from the part about him reading the contract. He'd signed it blindly, never thinking for a second the investment in professional photos wouldn't pay off big time and be instrumental in turning Nibbles around. He was certain the amazing images Toni delivered, along with the trendy redesign of the site, were sure to bring Nibbles' readers back in droves. His gamble had backfired, and his insistence on suing Toni for compensation was against his lawyer's explicit advice. He was running out of options and decided to give it one last shot.

"You're bluffing Toni, and we both know it. I'm prepared to make you an offer you can't refuse. I'll have my lawsuit dismissed and settle for two hundred fifty thousand. It's a one-time only opportunity. Ten thousand upfront today seals the deal. If you need to pay me the rest in installments, we can work out a payment plan.

How about if I come to your office right now and you write me a check? You can thank me then, huh?" He congratulated himself on his brilliance. *A very convincing performance, if I do say so myself,* he thought.

Toni had other ideas. He listened in dismay while she first of all laughed, then repeated her promise to report him to the police if he ever contacted her again. Her words drifted in and out of his head as anger washed over him. "I'm leaving on a trip tomorrow," she was saying, "…. never want to hear from you……see you in court……. leave me in peace."

The line went dead, and Tyler abruptly returned to his senses. *I'll leave you in peace, alright, and I mean everlasting peace,* he seethed, as he began to formulate a plan.

CHAPTER SEVEN

Al nudged a still sleeping Cassie on the shoulder. When she didn't stir, he shook her a little harder. "Wake up, sweetheart."

Cassie opened her eyes before blinking, closing them again, and rolling over.

Al stared at his wife and smiled at how peaceful she looked. It was a shame to have to wake her. He yanked the blankets off of her. "I hate to do this sleepyhead, but ya' gotta get up."

Cassie groaned. "What time is it?" She eyed the alarm clock on the nightstand before letting out an exasperated squeal. "Al, it's only 5:30 a.m. Go back to bed." She looked up to where Al was standing at the side of the bed looking down at her and swiped him away with her arm. "Stop pointing that gun at me. I'll get up if you promise not to shoot."

Al leaned over and kissed her, his face serious. "Hurry up. Red's done and gone missin'. I think he's been dognapped. I heard a noise, and when I went downstairs, the back door was lyin' open. No Red. He's disappeared without a trace." He waved his hands in the air, swinging the gun around. "Vamoose."

Cassie pulled herself into an upright position and rubbed the sleep from her eyes. "That doesn't sound like the Red I know. He wouldn't go anywhere against his will without putting up a fight. Are you sure you didn't leave the door open last night, and he's wandered outside? You'll probably find him sitting on the jetty by the sailboat or in the trees taking care of his morning business."

Al grunted. "I checked there already. Ima tellin' ya', Cassie, I think he's been clipped. Of course, I locked the door. Whaddya' take me for? This house is harder to get out of than a high security prison."

Cassie swung her legs over the side of the bed. "I can just see the headlines now. 'Canine Escapes from Alcatraz.' Maybe Red will get a movie deal."

Al was already heading for the stairs. "That's if we can find him. C'mon, there's no time to waste on small talk." His hulking frame descended the stairs two at a time, and he called out several times for Red, but the house was silent apart from the sound of Cassie complaining about having been dragged out of bed so early.

Cassie followed him downstairs and joined him in the kitchen. She walked over to where Al was sitting at the table with Red's half-full dog bowl in front of him. His finger was poised, ready to stick in the bowl.

"Al...what are you doing?" She moved the bowl out of his reach. "I'll make breakfast now. I know you're upset, but a proper healthy meal will be a lot more nutritious than kibbles."

When Cassie's back was turned, Al grabbed the bowl back again. He ran his finger around the rim, before placing the tip of his finger on the edge of his tongue and licking it gingerly.

"Nothin'," he muttered, before repeating the exercise. He looked up with a grin. Cassie was staring at him with her hands on her hips. "Tastes fine," he explained. "I can't detect traces of poison or anything else suspicious. I thought Red mighta been doped, but all I can taste is regular kibbles."

"Thank goodness for that." Cassie turned back to finish fixing the coffee. A few moments later she returned to the table with two steaming mugs. Al looked at Cassie, and then over at the open doors onto the patio, where a light drizzle of overnight rain had covered the outdoor furniture with a layer of moisture. Two pairs of rubber Crocs shoes and a pair of pruning shears lay abandoned beside the rosebushes he and Cassie had spent the last few evenings cutting back.

"It's my fault," he said, with a gloomy stare into the murky liquid in his mug. "I feel so guilty."

"Here, don't forget your vitamins." Cassie pushed two orange pills towards him, and he gulped them down with a chaser of coffee.

"If I hadn't made such a fuss over Balto when he was stayin' with us, Red wouldn't have felt left out. Now Red's gone off with some good-fer-nuthin', and I'll never get a chance to show him how much I care about him. I'll never forgive myself."

Cassie reached over and stroked his hand. "Red's a clever dog, just like his master. He's never doubted for a minute how you feel about him, of that I'm sure. He's just not needy for attention in the same way Balto was. Dogs are a bit like children. You end up focusing your attention on whichever one of them needs the most at the time. It doesn't mean you love your other children any less."

"Ssh." Al placed his finger to his lips and jumped up. He lifted his gun off the table, stepping nearer to the patio doors. The sound of footsteps was audible on the stone patio, and a woman's voice carried on the breeze. He peeked outside and heaved a sigh of relief at the sight of Hillary and Red rounding the side of the house. Hillary was talking animatedly to a contented looking Red, who was prancing alongside her on a leash.

Al lowered his gun as Hillary spotted him.

"Good morning, Al," she said, entering the kitchen and unclipping the leash from Red's collar. Red barked at the sight of his dog bowl on the table, and Al hastily returned it to its rightful place by the door.

"Hi Cassie," Hillary said. "I hope you two don't mind me taking Red out. I couldn't sleep, and Red was the only one awake when I came down earlier. We went to the beach, didn't we, Red?"

Red glanced up momentarily before returning his focus to the kibbles in his dish.

Al beamed. "Ima so happy to see ya' both. Thought we mighta' had an intruder who came an' stole Red away from under our noses." He pulled out a chair for Hillary. "Sit down and join us."

"Thanks, Al." Hillary pulled something from her pocket and set it on the table. "Here's the key for the patio doors. It was sitting on the counter. I forgot to lock them on my way out, but I figured it's so quiet around here it would be safe. I hope you weren't worried."

"Nah," Al said with a sideways glance at Cassie, who was smirking by the stove. "No reason to worry at all. How did you enjoy the beach in the dark? I think Red could find his way there blindfolded."

"I think you're right." Hillary chuckled. "We had a little bit of moonlight to help us along. It was so peaceful, just the sound of the water lapping on the shore. I was thinking of Toni, at one with the universe again. She wasn't religious, but she believed in a higher power. She always described it as a Oneness. At the beach, I kind of understood what she meant." She tucked a strand of her long blond hair behind her ear, struggling to hold back tears.

Al squeezed her hand wordlessly. They sat like that until Cassie broke the silence.

"Hillary, you're just in time for breakfast." Cassie carried another mug of coffee over to their guest. She nodded at the center of the table. "Help yourself to sugar and cream, and I'll be right back with some bacon and scrambled eggs. Al, you're on toast duty."

Al jumped up to his station by the toaster. "Yes, ma'am."

Over breakfast, the conversation returned to the subject of Toni's murder. Cassie spoke up. "Hillary, something's been bothering me that I wanted to run past you. It's about a man Toni mentioned a couple of times who had been causing her problems. He worked in her office building. I remember being at her office on the island when a janitor kept interrupting our meeting.

"He was rather abrupt, although Toni was very patient with him. She told me he bothered her all day long with petty issues relating to building maintenance which should have been none of her concern. She said she was finding it hard to get any work done with him around."

Hillary frowned. "Yes, she said something along the same lines to me as well. It was a bit of a running joke between us that Hector, that's the maintenance man's name, had a crush on her. In fact, he called her yesterday when she was working at home, and I teased her about it. He's asked her out a few times and pretty much wouldn't take no for an answer, even though she told him she was dating someone else."

Al grabbed the notebook and pen he kept at the side of the table. *Hector*, he scratched in his spidery hand. "Do we have a last name for this guy?"

Hillary shrugged.

"That's okay, I'll get Rob on it right away."

He started to get up, and Cassie pulled him back by the arm. "It's still early. Finish your breakfast, honey," she said softly. "Why not wait a while, and call him after 7:00 a.m.?"

Al glanced at the clock, and sheepishly sat down. "Yeah, I guess it can wait until then. I was wonderin', Hillary, about the man Toni had been seein', the Jace feller. What do you know about him?"

Hillary thought while she munched on a piece of toast. "His name is Jace Carson. Like I said last night, they met when Toni shot some pictures for a billboard ad for one of the television shows he produces. He loved the shots she came up with and started using her for other work. Then he asked her out for dinner. I remember Toni telling me she was reluctant to mix business with her personal life, but it was me who advised her to go for it."

"Why was that?" Al nodded to Cassie, who poured more coffee for him.

"Toni had one failed marriage, when she was very young," Hillary explained. "After that, she threw herself into work. I think she blamed herself for the marriage breakdown, but in reality, it was one of those things. She was young and foolish, and madly in love. She made a mistake. The marriage never should have happened, but she was headstrong and wouldn't listen to our mother's advice to wait. It lasted for a year, although they were on the rocks from right after the honeymoon."

"I swore I'd never get married," Al commented. "Until I met this woman here and fell head over heels." He turned to Cassie. "Sometimes ya' just gotta go with yer' heart. Right, sweetheart? And if it don't work out, Ima gonna bury ya' under the patio." He grinned.

"Somehow, the way the two of you are with each other, I don't think that's going to happen," Hillary continued with a wistful stare at them. "For years, Toni said she wasn't looking for love, but I could tell there was something missing in her life. The way she talked about Jace, I urged her to give him a chance. We were going to catch up on everything on our trip to Alaska. I sensed she had some news to tell me." She sniffed and paused to compose herself.

"Take yer' time," Al said. "What kind of news?"

"It's a guess, but I think they may have been thinking of moving in together, or even getting married. She'd mentioned selling her place, or remodeling and adding a room addition. Jace had been having issues with his ex, but Toni stood by him while he dealt with it. Her one concern about committing to someone was if they had baggage with someone else."

Al had covered the page of his notebook with doodles while Hillary was talking. He had scrawled *Jace Carson's ex* in large letters with arrows pointing to it.

Hillary glanced at the scribbles on the page and looked up at Al. "I suppose I should call Jace and let him know what's happened. I don't want him to find out from anyone else. Do you want me to ask him about his ex?"

Al shook his head. "No need. Ima gonna' get Rob on it now." His chair made a scraping sound against the floor as he abruptly stood up from the table. "Cassie, Luke should be done with his mornin' run and be on his way to the office. Ima gonna head straight down there." He kissed the top of her head.

Cassie smiled. "Go. Keep us informed. I'll stay here with Hillary."

Al picked up his gun and strode out the door to where the sun was rising just over the patio, whistling as he headed for his car.

CHAPTER EIGHT

Hector Delgado took a crescent wrench from his toolbox and twisted the shut-off valves located between the incoming water supply lines and the supply hoses for the sink faucet. Then he lifted the bucket he'd placed under the sink to catch the dripping water and poured the water that had collected inside it out the window. Snapping his tool box shut, he carried it back to the tiny storage room out in the hallway and left it there.

He suspected the leaking faucet he'd warned Toni about was part of a bigger plumbing problem for the whole building, but that did not concern him. He was only biding his time in this crummy job until something better came along, such as a night watchman position at one of the big chain supermarkets on the island. Better pay, and he could sleep on the job.

That'll have to do, he thought, scratching his head. *No water, no leak. No one else around here seems to care, so why should I?*

He lifted his backpack down from the hook in the storage room where it was hanging and grabbed his coat, confident his absence would not be missed if he knocked off early from his shift. He knew from his calls with her earlier that Toni was working from home, and her assistant Barrie hadn't shown up at the office either. Angela, the receptionist, was too busy filing her nails and giggling on the phone with her boyfriend to notice what was going on. If Big Foot himself walked in, she wouldn't bat an eye.

The building was empty apart from the rooms used by the Food Porn Photography business and the other part-time staff Toni employed on an ad hoc basis when they were needed if a shoot was in progress. He'd come back that evening and lock up. Angela would be none the wiser. *When the cat's away the mice...*

He whistled on his way out through the back door, sauntered down the alley, and around the corner. From there it was a ten-minute walk to the apartment he shared with the man he considered to be his brother, Diego. The fact they didn't share parentage was irrelevant to either one of them. Friends since childhood, they were astral twins, born on the same day and raised in the same Seattle district of Georgetown.

They walked to school together, learned to drive at the same time, and even shared girlfriends as teenagers. When Hector decided to move to Bainbridge Island, Diego insisted on coming along with him.

"For the adventure," Diego had said.

"It's not like I'm going far," Hector pointed out, but Diego's mind was made up.

Hector had a plan for the future, whereas Diego was a drifter with no plan other than to bounce along through life, one day at a time. Diego worked casual jobs here and there until he had some money, then he loafed around until his beer money was spent. When that happened, the same cycle would start all over again.

"You've sold out to the American Dream," Diego would mock Hector, who was saving for the down payment he'd need to make on a newly built condominium in an affordable development. "Who do you think you are, all clean-shaven and with the short haircut, huh? Forgotten your roots, have you?"

"No, but I'm an American, just like you," Hector had responded. "On the other hand, if you'd be happier as a street vendor staking out corners selling fruit drinks and snacks to tourists, why don't you go live in Mexico and embrace your roots there? You can hang out with the shopkeepers standing in the doors of their establishments, beckoning shoppers inside to look at the shelves brimming with tacky merchandise."

Hector knew Diego wouldn't go south of the border, even though he had family there. His friend was too lazy and too broke to make the trip.

"You're home early," Diego called from the sofa when Hector opened the front door of their apartment and stepped straight into the living and kitchen area, which was one tiny room. "You forgot to take out the garbage this morning," he added, with a laugh. "And you call yourself a janitor, huh?"

Hector set his backpack on the floor. "What are you, my wife or something? Move over, dude," he said, motioning for Diego to move his feet off the sofa. "Where am I supposed to sit?"

"The floor," Diego said, then laughed again before making room for Hector. "Did your boss let you leave early?" He clasped his hands together and beat his chest with them while screwing up his face. "Oh Toni, Toni, I love you, Toni."

Hector's face clouded over. "Stop with the funny stuff, Diego. She's not my boss. I work for the landlord, not her."

"Doesn't matter. She's still never going to go out with you, man. You've got to stop asking her. Hector Foolgado, that's you. Find yourself a nice Lupe from around here and have yourself some fun for a change."

Hector shrugged. "Just because you only date Hispanic ladies doesn't mean I have to." He fake-punched Diego on the arm. "I'm a hot-blooded lover, but I like all women, not just our kind. Nothing wrong with that, is there?"

"There is if you're not getting any action, my friend. When's the last time you…"

Hector ended the conversation by abruptly getting up from the sofa. "Got a cold one? Now seems like a good time." He walked over to the refrigerator and looked inside before turning back to Diego with a frown. "You drank all the beers? This is getting kind of old. I'm not your beer broker. Get off your butt and buy your own for a change."

"Geez, Hector. Chill, man. Some of the guys came by before lunch. We smoked a couple of joints and drank a few beers. You should try it, you know, try and relax for once. What's the biggie?"

Hector shook his head. "Get a life, bro." His eyes scanned the room. "You don't see it, do you? This place…" His voice drifted off as he looked around the apartment at the shabby sofa, the rug with a smattering of holes where it had been burned by falling cigarette ashes, the kitchen from another century. They were all reminders to Hector of how little he'd achieved and how far he still had to travel on his journey to success.

"You think this is all there is," Hector continued. "All you deserve. You're over thirty with no ambition. Not me, man. No way." He felt a rush of blood in his temples, and he balled up his fist, punching the kitchen countertop.

Diego stood up. "You think you deserve more, but why? Because you're better than me, is that it?" He raised his hand and shook a finger at Hector. "We're the same, you and me, no different. Since when did you forget your heritage? Your mama would roll over in her grave if she knew you were chasing after that white chick."

"Don't bring my mama into this," Hector growled. His mother, a nurse, had been one of the founding members of the Seattle Association for Hispanic Families. Funded entirely by donations, one of their primary causes was supporting underprivileged Hispanic families affected by serious illnesses and paying for healthcare when the family couldn't afford life-saving treatment. Even though Rosita Delgado died poor, her legacy lived on through the Association, which was championed by some high profile Hispanic celebrities.

Rosita's achievements were one of the reasons Hector had moved away from Georgetown. Although it was never discussed, he sensed his father's disappointment that he had yet to make anything of himself. Flunking out of high school without graduating wasn't a good start. When Hector saw his father, which wasn't often these days, he embellished the truth about his life to try and make his old man proud. The sadness in his father's eyes showed that Hector Sr. didn't believe him.

Diego wasn't letting it go. "Hit a raw nerve, did I? Let me spell it out for you, Hector, because you appear to be laboring under some sort of grand delusion. Aspirations are all well and good, but they won't change the color of your skin. They won't change your job prospects or where you're going to live. So, why not accept that and save yourself the trouble?"

"That's not true," Hector muttered. He'd read all the books on goal setting and visualization. *If you can dream it, you can achieve it* was one of his favorite daily affirmations.

"Buddy, I hate to break it to you, but it is. You have no qualifications, and you'll never earn enough to buy a condominium bigger than a shoebox that you'll be paying for until you're eighty. And Toni what's her face? She will never, ever, consider you worth dating. Girls like her don't date guys like us."

Guys like us. The words spun around inside Hector's head as he stared at Diego. Looking at his roommate, he suddenly saw himself through Toni's eyes. It didn't matter that Hector's hair was neatly cut while Diego's curled up on his collar. Or that Hector was clean shaven where Diego had a two-day-old stubble. The two men were the same age, recently turned thirty. They had the same olive-toned, swarthy skin. But as far as Toni Adams was concerned, they weren't good enough.

Something inside of Hector snapped. All his hopes and dreams came crashing down around him, and he gripped the countertop while his world started spinning. Diego was right. *Why didn't I see it before?*

"Are you okay?" Diego asked with a frown and a look of concern on his face. "You look kind of weird. Why don't you sit down, and I'll make us some coffee?"

Hector staggered towards the door. "I have to get out of here."

Diego tried to block him, reaching out to hold him back, but Hector sidestepped him.

"Hey, I'm sorry, bro," Diego said, following Hector as he walked towards the door. "I was out of line. Forget what I said, you know I'm full of…"

Diego's words never registered with Hector, who could only hear the thudding of his heartbeat whooshing in his ears as he slammed the door shut behind him.

His dignity was in tatters. Toni had never been anything but polite to his face, but now he was convinced she must have been laughing at him behind his back. He thought of his mother and was filled with an intense sense of pride in his background.

Hector Foolgado no more. Toni Adams will pay for how she's treated me, I'll make sure of it, if it's the last thing I do.

CHAPTER NINE

The first time Sophia Waters met Toni Adams, she liked her a lot. When Toni arrived on the set of the television show Sophia hosted carrying a box of mini-donuts and two Starbucks' caramel macchiatos, Sophia knew she'd found a kindred spirit.

"Welcome to 'Good Living in the Northwest'," Sophia said with a smile, reaching out her hand, into which Toni placed one of the Starbucks' cups. "You must be Toni?"

Toni grinned. "And you must be Sophia. I mean, of course you are. I recognize you from your show. I watch it every week." Her face turned crimson. "Who doesn't? Um," her voice faltered. "It's not like me to be lost for words. I guess I'm a bit starstruck, that's all. Do you like donuts?" She offered her the black and white box with a shaking hand.

"Like them?" Sophia opened the box and peered inside. She looked back at Toni with wide eyes. "Are you kidding me? They're my fatal weakness."

"Great," Toni said, relaxing. "Because these are from Taboo, you know that hot new place in Pioneer Square? They sell out by noon daily, but a friend of mine knows a guy…" She beamed. "Hey, you've got to grab the perks of the job when you can, right?"

Sophia nodded. "Right. First things first." She turned around to her assistant director and beckoned him over. "How are we doing for time, Johnno? Can you spare me for ten minutes?"

Johnno raised an eyebrow. "I might be able to." He eyed the black and white box which Sophia was holding out to him and selected a chocolate concoction, then moved away with a wink.

Ten minutes turned into thirty while Toni and Sophia bonded over glazed and frosted donuts laced with assorted gooey creme fillings. By the time Johnno came over to tell Sophia they really had to get back to shooting that week's show, the two women had discovered they knew several people in common and shared a love for tequila and Nicholas Sparks movies, in addition to their mutual weakness for donuts.

"Just pretend I'm not here," Toni instructed, when Sophia started the cooking segment of that week's show, and Toni had unpacked her equipment. "It's just another camera in the studio."

Sophia looked up from where she was trying to mix a roux and wrinkled her nose. "Yes, but the show gets edited to within an inch of its life. Even if I mess this up, a perfect dish will come out of the oven for the final cut. We have chefs behind the scenes duplicating everything I attempt to make. You, on the other hand, get to see my real efforts in all their lumpy detail."

"Don't worry," Toni assured her. "I promise I'll let you pick the final shots for the magazine profile."

True to her word, Toni had gotten Sophia involved in whittling down the final shots for the editorial piece in Celeb Cooking magazine. The issue turned out to be one of its biggest selling editions of the year, due to the cover image of Sophia with a dollop of runny chocolate sauce on her face and a half-eaten plate of lop-sided profiteroles on the table. With Toni's persuasion, Sophia had agreed to go public with her culinary imperfections and had won herself a whole new legion of fans in the process.

The women's paths had crossed several times since that first meeting, always in a work capacity, and they'd continued to enjoy easy-going professional banter on each occasion. One time, at a party for the opening of a new Scandinavian style restaurant in Ballard, they'd downed tequila shots at the bar while the other guests sipped pink champagne on the terrace.

That was why, when Sophia saw Toni on the arm of Jace Carson at the annual Northwest TV Awards, she did a double take, before freezing her out. On the night in question, Sophia was unable to dodge the attractive couple in time. She saw Toni wave at her and was headed in that direction before she realized her error. Only quick thinking and Sophia's professional training as an actress had saved her from utter humiliation when Toni and her companion approached.

"Toni, Jace," Sophia said smoothly, her smile never reaching her eyes. "Toni, don't you look ravishing, my darling!" She air kissed the space on either side of Toni's cheeks. "Love the dress, by the way. How brave of you to wear something off-the-rack for an event like this. I'm sure I saw your dress in Neiman Marcus in Bellevue, but that style only comes in the large sizes, right? Anyway, I passed in favor of this Armani number. Giorgio's been pleading with me to wear his stuff." She glanced down at her own shimmering frock.

Toni's smile wavered, and Jace spoke up. "You two know each other?"

"We've met," Sophia said, through gritted teeth. She turned her head to the side, pretending to scan the assembled guests, before flashing a smile at a random woman in the crowd. "Oops, excuse me, I see someone I really must speak to. There's an award with my name on it tonight, and I have to mingle."

Sophia bolted away without a backwards glance, her vision blurred by tears, unaware she'd left Toni and Jace standing open-mouthed. Only when she'd reached the Ladies room and bolted herself into a stall, did she allow her emotions free rein.

She left the event immediately after collecting her award, feigning a migraine, but not before texting her best friend, Cheree.

Emergency summit at The Nest, be there at 10:00 p.m. :(Soph x

Cheree's reaction to the news that Jace, Sophia's ex-boyfriend, had moved on with a new amour, was underwhelming. "Sophia, sweetie, it's been six months since you two broke up," Cheree said, sipping her Mojito cocktail through scarlet red lips. "You can't expect Jace to live like a monk. You always knew something like this would happen, right?"

"We were just taking a break from each other," Sophia wailed into her tequila. "He loves me, I know it." She scowled at her friend. "This is all your fault. You're the one who made me play it cool and not call him. Remember that night after we went to Dottie's Double Wide, and you put my phone in the freezer? Now he's going out with that chubby photographer with the cute freckles, who stabbed me in the back and stole my man. So much for the girl code, huh?"

Cheree sighed. "You thanked me the next morning for not letting you drink and dial. And as for this Toni woman, you told me about her before. I thought you liked her?"

"Exactly," Sophia hissed. "She played me. She's a sneaky piece of work, all right. I wonder how she got her claws into Jace." She slapped her forehead with the palm of her hand. "I get it now. She was probably hanging around the TV studios, using me as a cover."

"Sophia, hun, I think I should get you home. You've had too much to drink, and you're not thinking straight. How Toni and Jace met isn't the point. He's a free agent. And if Jace had no idea you guys knew each other, maybe Toni didn't know either. Did you consider that?"

"C'mon," Sophia slurred. "Don't gimme' that, babe. When me and Jace were together, the whole state of Washington knew about it."

Cheree frowned and leaned closer to her friend. "Let's go, Sophia. People are staring."

"No." Sophia motioned to the bartender. "Two tequila slammers, over here please."

When the bartender had lined up the drinks, Cheree watched Sophia pour salt onto the side of her hand, lick it off, down the two shots in turn, then stuff a wedge of lime in her mouth. While Sophia was sucking the lime and screwing up her face, Cheree settled the tab and dragged her out of the bar by the elbow.

After helping Sophia back to her apartment in downtown Seattle, Cheree tucked a blanket over her comatose friend, and tiptoed out.

*****

A week after the TV awards, Sophia was no closer to coming to terms with Jace having moved on from their relationship. The memory of how he'd looked so comfortable with Toni, an arm snaked around her waist, twisted like a knife inside her chest every time she thought about it. She considered going to his office, but her nerve deserted her. She didn't want to run the risk of him humiliating her and having to face the sympathetic faces of the people who worked for him.

There would be no rerun of the time in his office when he'd dumped her after she'd dropped by unexpectedly to see him at work. He'd closed the door to his office, sat her down, told her she was 'too needy,' and that he didn't want to see her any more. She didn't think any of his staff had heard the conversation, or her tearful pleading with him to reconsider, but she wasn't about to make the same mistake twice.

One evening, a few days after seeing Jace and Toni together at the Northwest TV Awards, and against Cheree's advice, she called him.

"Hey, Jace," she said in her sultriest voice, when he finally answered after her fourth call to him. "It was good to bump into you last week. Just wondering if you'd like to come over to my place some night soon? I could cook, and we'd have a chance to catch up."

She heard Jace sigh. "No, Sophia, that won't be happening. Listen, it was lovely to run into you too, but I'm with Toni now."

"Oh, I know, and Toni's so sweet," Sophia said with a laugh. "I don't mean anything too heavy. Just to talk, as friends. I think we have some unfinished business, and I hate seeing you make a mistake with Toni." Her heart raced, feeling him slipping out of her reach. "There are things you should know about her. Scary things. She's not what she seems."

Jace paused. "I know everything I need to know about Toni, thank you."

"But what we had, you and me, it was special, right? You can't just treat me like this, tossing me away when you're done and stamping on my heart. You led me on, you…"

"I love her, Sophia. What you and I had together was fun, but it was a two-month fling. I wish you all the best in the future. Goodbye."

The line went dead. Sophia stared furiously at the phone. *He hung up on me,* she raged to herself. *I wonder if Toni was there, listening, egging him on?*

She walked over to the kitchen drawer and took out a sharp knife before sitting down at the counter. Pulling up the sleeve of her sweater, she used methodical strokes to cut diagonal slits on the thin skin of her inner arm between the crook of her elbow and her wrist. The same patch of skin was already marred with criss-cross scars, and Sophia savoured the pain as she drew blood. She wondered what it would be like to hurt Toni, to make her feel the type of pain she had caused Sophia.

As her blood dripped slowly onto the counter, she also wondered if Toni's blood would be the same color as hers.

There was only one way to find out. At that moment, Sophia had a flash of clarity.

CHAPTER TEN

Al called ahead to see if either of his assistants had arrived in the office for the day. Rob answered the phone after two rings.

"Yo, it's Al." He looked at the clock on the dash. It was 6:52 a.m. Out of curiosity, he added, "What time do ya' start work, Rob? Kinda' early, ain't it? Ya' got a place to go to outside the office, don'tcha?"

Al realized he knew very little about Rob, apart from the fact he was always available when needed, as well as being the best researcher he'd ever come across. There had been times when Al was in the Mob when he could have done with the kind of intel Rob came up with in lightning speed. It might have gotten him and his former boss, Vinny Santora, out of all kinds of trouble.

"I've been here for a while," Rob said in a cheerful voice. "And yes, I do have a life, but thanks for asking."

Al grunted, while making a mental note to speak to Cassie about inviting Rob over to the house for dinner sometime. Not when they were in the middle of this investigation, but maybe after things had calmed down.

"Got us a murder case," Al said. "Wanna' put the pedal to the metal investigatin' it."

"Toni Adams, by chance? I just heard about it on the radio this morning. I passed by her street on the way here to work, and there was a large police presence outside the house."

"That's the one." Al swerved his car while taking his notebook out of his pocket. Navigating the narrow winding island roads with one hand on the steering wheel, he turned the pages of his notebook with the other, before placing the book on the passenger seat at the most recent page. "Call Luke and tell him to get into the office pronto. Ima gonna be with ya' in about fifteen minutes. In the meantime, I got a list of names I need ya' to get started on."

Al glanced sideways at his notes and reeled off the information he had on Ethan Doyle, Tyler Alexander, and the janitor named Hector. "Also, Toni was seein' a guy named Jace Carson. At this point he may or may not be a suspect, but wanna' get him checked out anyway. Ima more interested in an ex-girlfriend of his. Don't know her name, but she may have a grudge."

"Sure thing, Boss. I'll get right on it."

"Thanks, Rob. See ya' in a bit." Al punched Dan Hewson's number into his phone and waited for him to pick up. When the call was diverted to his voicemail, Al left a message.

"Hey, Chief, Al De Duco here. Just wanted to let ya' know Hillary Adams has hired me to investigate her sister's murder. I'd appreciate any help ya' can send my way. Maybe ya' can gimme' a call when ya' get this message." He was about to hang up when he added as an afterthought, "Oh, and I hope yer' head's not sore after the dinner last night." He chuckled. "Bye, Chief."

When he reached High School Road NE, Al pulled in at Bainbridge Island's nautical-themed Starbucks.

"Hi, Al." The barista greeted him with a smile. "What's it going to be? The usual for the three of you?"

"Yeah, Nessa, no one makes Bainbridge Blend flat whites like you do. Me an' the guys love 'em. And gimme' six of yer' biggest Chocolate Chunk muffins. Rob's gonna need a lot of sustenance today."

"Did you hear about the murder?" Nessa asked as she worked the coffee machine. "Toni Adams was a lovely woman. I'll miss her cheerful personality in here. She always had a good word for everyone."

"Yeah, it's terrible." Al scanned the room. He noticed several regulars he often saw at this time of the morning. A man he didn't recognize was sitting by the window. "Who's that?" he asked Nessa. "Isn't it a bit early for the tourist trade?"

"No idea," Nessa said with a shrug. "But he's been here since we opened at 4:30 a.m. He came in all wet, like he'd been out in the rain."

"Thanks, Nessa." Al picked up his order from the counter and walked out, taking note of the young man's appearance. He was wearing a pair of Clark Kent glasses and dressed in expensive designer clothes, albeit damp and crumpled. His handsome face was unshaven, and his agitation was evident from the way he was tearing apart the paper wrapper on his muffin, piece by tiny piece. A small pile of shredded paper and crumbs lay on the table in front of him.

It was a short drive to the office, where Al handed Rob a coffee and the bag of muffins. "Here. Don't say I don't look after ya'."

"Hope there's one for me." Al's other assistant, Luke, said as he walked in the door behind him, and Al nodded at the coffees on the table.

Luke picked up a cup, while Al pulled the newspaper out from under Luke's other arm. Toni's face was splashed all over the front page of the Seattle Times.

"Ima gonna' take this," Al said, turning towards his office. "Rob, lemme' know when ya' got somethin' on the names I gave ya' earlier.

Luke, you an' me gonna take a little trip to Toni's business when it opens. I need ya' to find out who's on her payroll, so we know what we're dealin' with. Rob's already checkin' out the guy I got a line on."

Luke nodded. "I'm on it."

In his office, Al spread the newspaper out on his desk and pressed the button on the remote control that turned on the television mounted on the opposite wall. The murder had gotten extensive coverage in the Seattle Times, which Al understood since Toni had done a lot of work for them, and the talking heads on the local TV news channels were all over the murder case. He spent the next couple of hours sifting through and making notes on all the information and theories shared in the press and on TV, which ranged from a burglary gone wrong to a crime of passion.

He glanced up as Luke came in. "Whaddya' got?"

Luke sat down in the chair on the other side of Al's desk. "Toni had several members on her staff. The receptionist, Angela, is a ditsy teenager in her first job since she graduated from Bainbridge High School. She was the senior prom queen, dated the captain of the football team, likes puppies. You get the picture."

Al raised an eyebrow. "Squeaky clean?"

"I wouldn't go that far, but I reckon she's harmless. Did I mention her father's the Mayor?"

"Gotcha'. Who else?"

Luke checked his notes. "A couple of temps, who worked on a part-tine basis during busy periods and when Toni had important jobs she needed help with. Toni looked after them well, and paid them more than the going rate, so they were very loyal to her."

Al raised an eyebrow. "There's gotta be someone who didn't like her, or we wouldn't be havin' this conversation. Is that it?"

"One more. The next person's more interesting." Luke leaned in and said, "Barrie Jones was Toni's assistant. They worked together for over five years. Barrie's not popular with the rest of the staff, who call her Shark Lady. From what Rob tells me, Barrie's boyfriend, some guy named Jim, made an offer to buy Toni's business not that long ago. He got a 'Thanks, but no thanks' in reply. Shark Lady wasn't too happy about that."

"I see." Al noticed Rob stick his head around the door, and called him in. "Good work on those people, Rob. What about the others?"

Rob came over and stood next to Luke. "The janitor's name is Hector Delgado."

Al scratched his head. "The name sounds familiar. Is he any relation of the woman who did all the campaignin' to fund healthcare for Hispanic families a while back?"

Rob nodded. "Yep. His mom was Rosita Delgado. He's a member of a few Hispanic Rights groups himself, although he's not been very active in them the past few years. I have a contact who can infiltrate one of the groups and get us more info on him. It's a male-only militant group, and they're rumored to be behind some offensive smear campaigns against local politicians. As far as violence goes, there's solid evidence of that as well."

"In that case, we can assume Hector knows some nasty people," Al said. The TV news was over, and the theme tune of a daytime soap opera filled the room. He clicked the remote control to switch off the television set. "That's better. Now I can hear myself think." He looked at his notebook. "Ethan Doyle?"

Rob shook his head. "I need more time to find out where he's living these days. My contacts in Key West are still looking into it. Same with running a check on Jace Carson's ex-girlfriends. It's not a long list, so if a person of interest becomes apparent, I should know about it pretty quick." He handed Al the pile of paperwork he was holding.

"No problem." Al tapped his pen on the desk with an amused smile. Even when Rob didn't have all the answers, he always knew someone who could get them. Al admired Rob for never naming his sources. Smart guy. He had a lot of respect for both of the young men who were in his office. "Thanks again, Rob."

Rob turned to leave. Al was flicking through the sheaf of papers and said, "Rob, wait a minute. Think that still leaves that blogger dude, Tyler Alexander, right?"

"Sorry. Yes, you're right." Rob scratched his head. "That printout must have gotten pushed into another pile. In a nutshell, Tyler is a very angry man. He's clashed with almost all of the companies who advertised on his blog. I'm not sure if it's been medically diagnosed, but from what I hear, his behavior is very symptomatic of PTSD.

"He was never in the armed services, but one of the advertisers said his own brother had been in Iran and when he returned from combat, he acted very similarly to Tyler. I'll get the papers for you now."

Al got up. "That's okay, I think we got plenty to be goin' on with." He nodded at Luke. "What say you an' me pay a visit to Food Porn Photography, buddy?"

Luke scrambled up from his seat. "Let's go. I'm driving."

"Nope. Ima gonna' drive. Yer' way too slow," Al said, enjoying the bickering match that ensued the whole way down the stairs and out onto the street.

CHAPTER ELEVEN

Cassie looked up as Hillary entered the kitchen. "Those smell delicious," Hillary said, admiring the cookies Cassie had just taken out of the oven and was placing on a wire rack.

"My baking's average, but Al likes them." Cassie smiled. "You can try one when they cool down." She watched Hillary pull out a high kitchen stool and sit opposite where she was standing at the counter. The young woman's eyes were sunken, and her skin was pale, despite her natural tan. "Did you speak to Jace?"

"Yes. I'm glad it was early and before he left for work, or he would have heard about the murder through the media. He said he never watches television at home, because it's his job and otherwise he'd never escape from it." She shuddered and closed her eyes for several seconds before staring back at Cassie like a wounded animal.

"It was awful. He said he'd spoken to Toni yesterday and wasn't expecting to hear from her again for a few days, since he knew we were taking a trip. He'd texted her on his way home from work, but it was late when he got out of his meetings, so again he thought nothing of it when she didn't reply."

Cassie dusted some powdered sugar on top of the cookies. "How did he seem?"

Hillary's eyes widened. "You mean, was he upset? He sounded kind of…stunned, is how I would describe his reaction. He became very quiet, and when he spoke I could hear and feel the emotion in his voice. He said it would take some time for him to process the dreadful news, and how his life would never be the same again. I know what he means." As Cassie watched helplessly, she buried her head in her hands and began to sob.

"How about if I make us some coffee," Cassie said, "and you can try out one of the cookies. I know it's not the same, but when my children were upset when they were little I always gave them warm milk and cookies. When you're ready, we can talk about who else you need to call and what practical matters I can help you with. Or maybe you'd prefer to lie down for a while? You're going to need all of your strength to get through the next few days."

The memory of her first husband's death a year earlier was still fresh in Cassie's mind. Despite her happiness with Al, a different piece of her heart would always belong to Johnny Roberts. The period following his murder while he was on a golf outing in Whistler, British Columbia, remained a blur to her. She knew she'd only made it through the aftermath of his murder with the help and support of her family and friends. Hillary had no family left, and Cassie's heart went out to her.

Hillary looked up and blinked through her tears. "I think a cookie is just what I need." She wiped her cheeks. "Would you excuse me for a few minutes? I just want to get freshened up."

"You got it. Take your time."

Cassie was sitting on the patio when Hillary returned a short while later. The earlier rain had cleared and made way for a cool but bright day, and every now and then a gust of wind blew the first leaves of fall onto the lawn. From where he stood on the top step of the patio, Red surveyed his outdoor kingdom.

It was the spot which offered the best vantage point of the vast garden, which was bordered by the expanse of water at the far end that was Puget Sound, tall pine trees, and shrubbery marking the boundary with Dino Argyros' home next door.

Cassie was pleased to see Hillary looking better when she joined her outside. Color had returned to their guest's freshly washed cheeks, and she'd fixed her hair into a loose bun. In place of the jogging pants she'd been wearing earlier were attractive jeans and a striped sweater. Around her neck on a strap hung a heavy camera with a protruding lens.

Cassie poured the coffee and held out the plate of cookies to Hillary, whose eyes lit up. "I warned you, I'm an amateur baker, so don't get too excited," Cassie said.

"This sounds weird, but do you mind if I take a photo first?" Hillary pressed a button on the camera and the lens began extending. "It's such a gorgeous setting, and these cookies, with a bloom placed just here…"

Before Cassie could reply, Hillary had grabbed the plate of cookies. In no time, she had styled them on the table in an arrangement with the coffee pot and mugs, a few brightly colored fall leaves that had blown onto the stone patio floor, all superimposed against the natural backdrop of flowering pink echinaceas growing in the background. The camera clicked as Hillary began snapping rapid shots from different angles, her concentration evident. When she was done, she sat down and grabbed a cookie.

"Thanks," she said, starting to munch. By way of explanation she added, "Photography's a hobby of mine. I'm nowhere near as good as Toni was, obviously, but we both learned at the same time when we took a photography course together. Toni made a business out of it, and I take my own pictures for my real estate listings. The food porn thing of taking photographs of various food items is addictive."

"I can see you've got an eye for setting up a shot," Cassie said. "You know…" She trailed off, checking herself. "Sorry, never mind."

Hillary sipped her coffee. "Please, go on. I won't be offended."

"I'm not sure if you're aware of it," Cassie said, "but Toni and I were collaborating on a charity cookbook, using recipes from local chefs. Toni was taking the pictures. If yo—"

"I'll do it." Hillary's face broke into a smile. "I'd be honored and humbled to be involved." She reached out to Cassie and grabbed her hand. "Thank you. This means so much to me, you have no idea. To be a part of Toni's legacy. Oh no, I think I'm going to cry again."

Cassie handed her a tissue. "Here, take this. Don't worry, I came prepared." She nodded at the packet of Kleenex behind the coffee pot.

Hillary sniffed and blew her nose. Red came trotting over to her side and licked her hand. She gently stroked his fur as she spoke to Cassie. "I've decided I need to keep busy. Sitting around here crying isn't going to do anyone any good, and it's not going to help catch whoever killed my sister. As well as making the arrangements for Toni's funeral and sorting out her affairs, I can make myself useful for as long as I'm here."

"Good for you." Cassie thought for a second. "You know, it would do you a lot of good to talk to Luke. He works for my husband, and he's also my daughter's boyfriend. His fiancée was murdered not that long ago, and he's coped extremely well. One of the things he said that helped him was taking action. It was a huge effort for him to move on with his life instead of living in limbo. But ultimately, he didn't want the killer to win by succeeding in taking away his life as well."

"That sounds like a good attitude," Hillary said. She downed the last of her coffee and straightened up. "I'm going to go to Al's office and volunteer my services in the investigation. Can I ask a favor?"

"Of course." Cassie smiled, anticipating Hillary's question with a sense of déjà-vu.

"Would it be alright if I take Red with me today? I could do with the company, and we get along really well together."

"I think Red would like that a lot. Oh, and if I bag up some cookies would you take them with you to Al's office? His assistant Rob has a sweet tooth, and Luke never refuses a home-baked treat either. My daughter, Briana, doesn't have a culinary bone in her body." Cassie rose from her seat and started to walk into the kitchen.

"I know the feeling." Hillary jumped up and followed her inside, Red not far behind.

CHAPTER TWELVE

Al pulled into the parking lot of the building where Toni's Food Porn Photography business had been based since she'd moved to Bainbridge Island several years earlier. It was a dockside block of units in a quiet commercial area overlooking Eagle Harbor. Although many local businesses had moved to the new business center on the island that had created a lot of buzz with its co-working spaces, trendy interiors, and discounted leases for new tenants, Al much preferred this waterfront location with its view of the boats and the skyline of Seattle in the distance.

Not dissimilar to the area where Jake's private investigation office was situated, it was tucked away from the bustle of downtown Winslow while still being within walking distance to the bank, post office, shopping areas, and the ferry terminal.

He stared out the window while he was waiting for Luke to wrap up a call with Rob. "Sure, we can wait," Luke was saying. "Tell Hillary to come on over. We're only a couple of minutes away. Al's just casing the joint."

Al grunted. "I'm admirin' the vista." He pulled the key from the ignition and opened the car door, climbing out and looking around.

Luke got out of the passenger side and grinned. "And checking all possible entrance and exit routes, if I'm not mistaken?"

"Kerrect-a-mentay. Yer' learnin'."

Al strolled over to the harbor edge and spent some time surveying the boats bobbing on the water. A large sailboat caught his eye. "Look at that beauty," he called to Luke, pointing at the sixty-five-footer. At the sound of panting and feeling a familiar weight brush against his leg, he looked down with a smile.

"Hey, Red. Yer' just in time, buddy. It's a 1968 Derecktor Ketch. Imagine the adventures we could have on that, huh? We'll come back and look at it a little closer another time." He turned to see Hillary walking towards them.

"You must be Luke," Hillary said, shaking Luke's hand. "I'm Hillary Adams, Toni's sister." She turned to Al. "I met Rob back at the office, and he said I'd find you both here. Have you been inside yet?"

Al shook his head. "No, let's go." He turned and began to walk towards the entrance. "We'll meet the staff and take a look around, got it? Jes' follow my lead." When they reached the door, Al stopped and gave a command to Red. "On guard." Looking up at Hillary, he winked. "Anyone tryin' to get outta' here in a hurry ain't gonna get far with Red blockin' their way." He stood back. "Do ya' want to go in first? They know ya'."

Hillary nodded, and stepped inside through the glass entry. At the reception desk, a pretty teenager with curly bangs was talking to a woman in her thirties with scraped-back hair and acne-scarred skin. The women looked over in surprise when they saw Hillary and her companions enter.

Al observed the young girl's face crumple. She jumped up from behind the desk and ran across the lobby. "Hillary, I…"

Hillary met her with outstretched arms, and both women began to sob. "Oh, Angela," Hillary said, stroking the girl's hair. "Just let it all out."

The other woman's eyes narrowed. She gave Al and Luke a frosty look and a curt greeting. "Hello, I'm Barrie Jones. I take it you're both friends of Hillary's?" She said Hillary's name like it left an unpleasant taste in her mouth.

Al stared at her through his sunglasses. As soon as they walked in, Al could tell she was a plain woman with a rough edge from the way her eyes had narrowed and her lip curled up. He sized her up in a few seconds, having known many others like her over the years. Regardless of whatever her position in life was now, it was obvious to Al that she'd had a hard start in the world. He stuffed his hands in his jeans pockets and looked around the lobby. She glared at him, jutting her chin out, and he paused a while longer before replying.

Let her sweat, he thought to himself. *What's she hidin'?*

When he decided he had let her squirm for long enough, he spoke up. "I'm Al De Duco, and this here's Luke Robertson." He motioned his head towards Luke, then cleared his throat. "We've been retained by Hillary in connection with the investigation into the murder…" His words hung in the air, and Hillary and Angela also turned to listen. "Of her sister, Toni Adams."

Barrie swallowed. "I see." She forced a nod at Hillary. "It's terrible news, we're all devastated. You have my utmost sympathy." Her tone was businesslike as she continued, "In fact, it's good you're here, since we weren't sure how to proceed. In the absence of any direction otherwise, I've instructed everyone to carry on as usual. I'm sure that's what Toni would have wanted. We have a shoot this afternoon at one of the Seattle magazines that's doing a special on the best dishes in Seattle. Don't worry, I have it covered."

Hillary remained silent and looked to Al for direction.

"Tell ya' what," Al said. "How about we all have a little staff meetin'? That way, Hillary can tell ya' herself what Toni woulda' wanted, don'tcha think?"

"Very well," Barrie said, coming out from behind the desk.

"Please, follow me." She led them to a bright conference room with a table in the center surrounded by a half a dozen chairs. There was a whiteboard on the wall, and dirty cups on the table from a previous meeting. Barrie made no attempt to clear the cups, and stood with her arms folded while Luke, Hillary, and Angela sat down.

Al remained standing beside Barrie, towering above her. "Is Hector here today?" he asked.

She shook her head. "No. He called in sick."

"Fine," Al said. "Anyone else?"

"No," Barrie said. "We have two temporary staff members, but I'm meeting them in Seattle later for the shoot."

Al pulled out a chair and sat down. All eyes were on Barrie.

"Whaddya waitin' fer?" Al asked, pointing to the seat beside him. Wordlessly, she sat down.

Hillary began to speak, her voice soft and calm. Looking at Barrie and Angela in turn, she gave them a reassuring smile. "Barrie, I think you're right. We have to be professional. Toni wouldn't want to let anyone down, so if there are photography jobs already booked, I'd be grateful if you could cover them with the other staff members you have on call.

"However, if that's not possible, I'm sure clients will understand under the circumstances. If that happens, we need to make sure any monies are reimbursed for deposits that have already been paid. Who looks after the bookkeeping and banking?"

"I do," Barrie snapped.

If Hillary was bothered by Barrie's hostility, she didn't show it. "I'll need the computer passwords and access to all of the business records and files. You have my personal word that everyone's wages will continue to be paid as usual. I don't want anyone worrying about money. And I'd like the key to Toni's office, so I can remove her personal effects."

Barrie glared at Hillary. She fished in her pocket before pushing a key across the table to Hillary with a scowl. "Listen, let's cut to the chase. I have a question, and I'd like a straight answer," Barrie said with obvious concern in her voice.

"Of course," Hillary said.

"Is the business being sold, or what are your plans? You can't leave Angela, me, and the others just standing by, wondering about the future. If I'll be getting my notice, I'd just as soon leave now. On the other hand, if the business is for sale, I might be interested in making an offer."

Al straightened in his seat, fascinated by the turn the conversation had taken. Barrie's words were feisty, but her body language was saying something else. Under the table, he could see her sweaty hands fidgeting.

Hillary didn't skip a beat. "Barrie, no decisions have been made, but when they are, you'll be the first to know. And if the business is being sold, I'd be happy to give you first refusal at the market price."

"You would do that?" Barrie's eyes widened. "Thanks Hillary, I really appreciate it."

Hillary nodded, turning to Angela. "If you need some time to process this, why don't you go home, sweetie? That's if Barrie can spare you."

Angela shook her head. "It's okay. I'll stay. I'd like to help in any way I can. Whatever I can do, just let me know."

Hillary reached over and squeezed her hand. "Good girl. How about you show me Toni's office and then make all of us some coffee?"

Al interrupted. "Good idea. Luke, you go with Hillary and Angela. Barrie and I will just finish up in here."

Luke nodded, and Al watched the three of them leave the room. When they'd gone, Barrie bit her lip and looked at the door.

"Considerin' makin' a run fer it?" Al chuckled. "Ya' can try, but I wouldn't advise it."

He cracked his knuckles. "Now then, let's do story time. 'Cuz there's somethin' I think yer' not sayin', and I don't like it when people try to hold things back from Uncle Al."

Barrie shifted awkwardly in her seat. "I'm not sure what you mean."

Al smiled. "I'll start." He folded his arms. "Once upon a time, there was a mean, nasty woman by the name of Barrie Jones. She was jealous of her boss, Toni Adams, a popular woman who everyone loved. Do you want to finish the story, Barrie, or shall I?"

Barrie's face crumpled, and she began to cry.

*****

In Toni's office, after Angela had brought them coffee and left again clicking the door closed, Hillary turned to Luke. "What now?" she whispered. "Toni's everywhere. I feel like she's about to walk through the door any second and say 'Surprise!'"

Food pictures and framed magazine covers lined the walls. Dotted around the room on the desk and on the computer were yellow and pink sticky notes with memos scribbled on them with a black Sharpie. 'Call Jace'. 'Buy peanut butter.' Hillary unpeeled one from the top of a pile of cookbooks on the desk, her eyes filling with tears. "Hillary birthday card," she read aloud. Slumping into Toni's chair, she buried her head in her hands. "I don't think I can do this," she moaned.

Luke took control. "Sure, you can, Hillary. I know it's hard, but there might be something here that will lead us to Toni's killer." His eyes scanned the room. There was a filing cabinet in the corner, and some shelves containing a stack of file boxes. He walked over and picked up one of the file boxes, emptied out its contents, and handed the box to Hillary. "You can use this for any of Toni's personal effects that you want to take with you. I'll take a look at the computer, then make a start on the paperwork."

Hillary stared at the box and sighed. "What are you looking for?"

Luke shrugged. "I have no idea. There might be an email, a sticky note with a phone number on it, a customer complaint…or there could be nothing here of any use to us at all. We never know until we check it out."

Hillary rubbed her forehead. "And if there's nothing?"

"Then we keep looking. At her house, at her gym, in her car. You name it. We speak to her friends, her clients, her hairdresser, the assistant at the grocery store, anyone whose path might have crossed with Toni's in the period before her death. We don't stop until we get a lead. And we will get one, I promise you. What I can't promise is how long that might take."

Hillary opened one of the drawers on the side of Toni's desk.

Pens. A pack of gum. Headache pills. A bottle of perfume - Beach, by Bobbi Brown. She lifted the glass bottle and pulled off the lid, spritzing it into the air. Toni's signature scent of sand jasmine, seaspray, and mandarin filled the room. Rather than finding it upsetting, it had a relaxing effect on Hillary and she replaced the lid, setting the bottle on its side in the file box. It was soon joined by a pair of silver earrings, a lipstick, a CD, some fluffy socks, and a journal.

Reaching her hand to the back of the drawer to make sure she hadn't missed anything, Hillary pulled out two envelopes. Both were opened and addressed to Toni in the same handwriting. She turned them over, hesitant to read her sister's personal mail. Taking a deep breath, she pulled a folded page from one of the envelopes, opened it and scanned its contents. Her hand began to shake.

"Hillary, are you all right?" Luke was staring at her with concern.

She pulled the second letter from its envelope and read it in silence before handing both of them to Luke. Holding her hand over her mouth, she tried to hold back the bile that was burning the back of her throat. But her attempt was futile, and she bolted from Toni's office and broke into a run towards the bathroom.

CHAPTER THIRTEEN

Al was loitering down by the harbor with Red when he saw Luke approach, followed by a downcast Hillary.

"I found these in the desk of Toni's drawer," Hillary said, handing Al the two envelopes. "They're letters to Toni from our stepfather, Ethan Doyle. It seems he had designs on Toni's affections and was trying to meet up with her."

Al turned the envelopes over in his hand. The first, dated over a month earlier, had a Florida postmark and return address. Although the second, dated only the previous week, had no return address, its smudged black postmark indicated it had been mailed in Seattle.

"Okay if I read 'em?" he asked Hillary, who was crouching down and stroking Red.

She nodded. "Be my guest."

The letters were written in a scrawled hand. The first was almost poetic in its contents, and Al had to hold back a snort of laughter as he read it.

"Who does this guy think he is, that famous poet, Robert Browning?" he said. "Ethan's been stealin' a few lines from him, even if he's paraphrasin'. *'I would not change one word, one look...you are perfect to me."*

"I think Ima gonna' throw up." He frowned as he continued down the page and began to shake his head before looking over to Hillary. "Is this dude for real?"

"It's all garbage," she said. "All that stuff about 'I know you feel the same way.' Toni despised Ethan. She couldn't bear to be anywhere near him. She moved to Washington to escape the pain of watching him ruin our mother's life. It wasn't because of any unrequited love on Toni's part for Ethan, like he wrote.

"I can tell you categorically that I know that man made her skin crawl. The worst thing was, Mom met Ethan online. Toni helped her set up her dating profile and showed her how to 'wink' at men she liked. Toni blamed herself for ever suggesting the online dating thing."

The first letter, although cringeworthy, was harmless enough in its contents. It begged Toni to consider meeting Ethan to talk about their 'unfinished business.'

"'*I swear I am devoted to you…*'," Al read aloud, "*…'and if you will just give me a chance, I will show you happiness beyond your greatest dreams. Please, do not be swayed by guilt. It was your mother's dying wish for you to love and be loved. She made me promise to look after you, but I needed no encouragement. Please, set aside your doubts and follow your heart…*' Ugh." Al made a face and opened the other envelope.

The second letter was shorter and more disturbing.

Dear Toni

I am disappointed you have not shown me the courtesy to reply to my earlier correspondence or return my calls. Your display of bad manners would have been a terrible disappointment to your mother.

It does not surprise me, however, and I want you to know that I forgive you. Since you refuse to talk to me, I can only deduce you are still conflicted by your feelings for me and your loyalty to your family. I've decided to make it easy for you.

The next time you see me could be sooner than you think. You owe me the decency of sparing me a few moments of your time, Toni, for the years I selflessly gave your mother. We can talk, but if we get carried away and one things leads to another, don't be surprised. Trust me, when I show you the true meaning of love, your life will never be the same again.

Yours in anticipation,

Ethan

Al scratched his head and looked up at Hillary. "Wow. Apart from the guy being delusional, did he ever show any signs of violence, or an angry temper? Like towards your mother?"

Hillary thought for a second. "Ethan's a creep, that's a given. He never raised a hand to my mother as far as I'm aware, but he could be mean and moody. Kind of like a spoiled child. He was used to getting what he wanted."

Al turned to Luke. "Get back to Rob and see if he's been able to track down Ethan Doyle yet. We know Ethan was in Seattle when the letter was mailed a week ago. Maybe what Toni said about seein' him outside her house was true. Chances are, he's still around. Meantime, I jes' spoke to Chief Hewson. He said his men are finished at Toni's place, and we can have access to anything we want. That includes her cell phone, which they left at the house."

Luke nodded. "I'll call Rob now. How did your conversation go with Barrie Jones?"

"It was interestin', but I think we can rule her out of our inquiries. Turns out Barrie had a guilty conscience, but not because she murdered Toni."

"What did she say?" Hillary asked.

Al began walking back towards the parking lot. Luke, Hillary and Red fell into step beside him.

"Like I thought, Barrie Jones grew up on the wrong side of the tracks," Al explained. "She turned her life around when she moved to Seattle and met a guy, Jim Nolan, who taught her photography. Accordin' to Barrie, Jim is also the love of her life."

"Sounds about right," Hillary said. "I've never met him, but Toni had told me that Barrie had a long-term relationship with some man."

"She tol' me how Jim lined her up for a job with Toni, and how Toni had been very good to her over the years. She gave Barrie a lotta' responsibility and helped her make contacts in the industry." Al looked over at the office building. Barrie was standing watching them from her smoking spot out front. He raised a hand to her in a wave, and she nodded back.

"Barrie started off as a good worker," Al said, "but as time went on she became more and more embittered by Toni's success and popularity. When I pressed her, she admitted to wishin' harm on Toni so that she and Jim could take over the business. In fact, Jim had already made Toni an offer to buy Food Porn Photography, but Toni turned it down."

"I didn't know that," Hillary said. "And to think I just offered her first refusal if the business is being sold. I'm inclined to give her a piece of my mind." She swung around, but Al held her back.

"Let it go," he said gently. "Barrie's problem is insecurity. She considered foul play as a solution for Jim to be able to buy the business, because she wanted a reason to make it difficult for Jim to leave her. As it turns out, it's too late for that. Jim told her a coupla' days ago he was breakin' up with her." He paused, pressing his key fob to unlock his car. There was a loud click and the lights flashed as the central locking system on his Aston Martin disengaged.

"She'd decided to throw herself into bein' a good employee

instead and was gonna ask Toni when she got back from vacation if there was a possibility of becomin' a partner in the future. But now, after what's just happened, Barrie doesn't think she could raise the money to buy the business anyway. She's pretty upset."

"I see." Hillary glanced over her shoulder. "I guess me yelling at her won't achieve anything. Shall I follow you to Toni's place?"

"Yeah," Al said, opening the driver's door and getting into his car. He smiled at Red, who was still standing beside Hillary. "Looks like Red wants to go with you, if you don't mind."

"My pleasure." Hillary opened the door of Toni's car and Red jumped up onto the back seat while Luke got in the front passenger seat.

*****

At Toni's home, Hillary handed Al the key for the heavy front door, and Al entered first. "We can leave at any time," he said to Hillary with a reassuring smile. "Jes' say the word."

She nodded and stepped inside after him.

"I'm going to call Rob," Luke said, still standing on the steps. "I'll be there in a sec. And if you're looking for Red, he's wandered off into the garden."

Al made his way down the hallway, and when he reached the kitchen he held out his arm behind him to indicate to Hillary not to come any closer. "Jes' a moment," he said, taking another couple of steps towards the great room. The door was ajar, and a quick peek inside told Al all he needed to know. He clicked the door firmly shut. "You ain't goin' in there," he said to Hillary. "If it's okay with you, I'll ask Rob to arrange for the room to be stripped and cleaned."

Hillary raised a hand to cover her mouth and turned away with a nod. Al followed her gaze to the family photos adorning the walls. Her eyes rested on one of her and Toni wearing evening dresses.

"You both look pretty," Al said, stepping beside her. "Was it a party?"

"My mother's second wedding," Hillary said, her voice a monotone. "It broke up the family. It's hard to believe only a year earlier, my father was alive and well and everything was perfect. The cancer got him quickly, and he only survived a few months after his initial diagnosis. As soon as Mom married Ethan, Toni moved away, and I barely saw Mom even though I lived nearby. I don't blame her, though. It was Ethan's fault, not hers."

"That's sad," Al said. He didn't want to upset Hillary further by pointing out her mom was a grown woman who had a mind of her own, because he knew things were not always that straightforward. Controlling men had a way of isolating women, making them vulnerable and unable to stand up for themselves.

Just then Luke came through the front door and walked down the hallway. Al turned to Hillary and said, "Me and Luke are gonna' take a look around down here and see what we can find. Do ya' wanna' go upstairs and check out Toni's bedroom?" Seeing her face crumple, he reached into his pocket and handed her a handkerchief.

"I'll call you if I find anything," Hillary said, wiping the tears from her eyes. "And thanks," she said, blowing her nose into the handkerchief before making her way up the staircase, quietly sobbing.

Al reached for Toni's phone which was sitting on the hallway table. "Ima gonna' start with this and make a list of Toni's recent calls and texts. Luke, the kitchen's down there. I'm sure ya' can find the coffee before ya' do anything else."

Luke grinned. "You got it."

Al was still in the middle of logging Toni's telephone calls when he heard Hillary yell for him from upstairs. He bounded up the narrow staircase and found her sitting on the edge of a bed in a room with a triangular-shaped sloped ceiling. Stepping over the neatly-packed open suitcase on the floor and a pair of shoes lying on the rug, Al walked over to where Hillary was holding out a piece of paper, her eyes shining.

"This was on the nightstand," she said, handing him a handwritten to-do list. "I found it beside the photo of Toni and Jace."

Al looked at the framed photograph beside the bed, in which a beaming Toni and a grinning man with his arm around her were standing beside a stream, dressed in waterproof jackets and wearing rain boots.

Glancing at the note Hillary had handed him, he read it aloud as Luke appeared in the doorway. "Here we go. 'One,'" he said. "'Need to talk to Barrie and tell her that if she keeps up with the attitude, maybe she should look for another job.' I guess that ties in with what Barrie was sayin' to me earlier. She knew she'd been slackin' and Toni was on to her."

He gazed back down at the page. "'Two. Tell Tyler I know about him trying to destroy my creditability with the Northwest Food company. My lawyer says it's slander.'" He looked up. "Sounds like Rob was right about him, too. As well as the legal dispute Hillary mentioned, Tyler musta' been bad mouthin' Toni to other clients."

A sad smile crossed his face as he read the last item and looked over at Hillary.

"Wow. 'Three. Tell Jace yes, yes, yes!!!' Think that means she was gettin' serious with this Jace dude?"

Hillary's voice was barely a whisper. "Uh-huh."

Al rubbed his chin. "We need to talk to Jace. If he and Toni were that close, maybe he knows somethin'. Unless Rob has any reason to think otherwise, Jace ain't a suspect. Whaddya' think?"

"Let's go," Luke said.

Hillary started to stand up, but her knees buckled, and she slipped back onto the bed.

"Luke, help Hillary downstairs and drive her back to my place," Al instructed. "Ima gonna' meet ya' there. I jes' need to finish up here and call Jace to ask him to see us."

He waved a finger at Hillary, who had opened her mouth to protest. "No arguments. Al's da' boss."

CHAPTER FOURTEEN

"I don't think Hillary's happy about not coming with us to see Jace." Luke said as he gripped the inner door handle while Al floored the accelerator of his Aston Martin and sped down the driveway.

In his rearview mirror, Al could see Cassie standing at the doorway of their house with her arm around Hillary, watching them drive off. "Yeah, but Hillary's in no state of mind to go anywhere. She's been runnin' on adrenaline all day. She was up walkin' Red before dawn, so I was right to insist she stay home with Cassie and rest a while."

"I'm not saying you're not right," Luke said. "But Hillary was asking me when we were in Toni's office earlier how I coped after Megan was murdered. I told her keeping busy was the only way I stayed sane. Does leaving her back there, knowing how helpless she must feel, make me a hypocrite?"

Al grunted. "Ya' worry too much. Jes' think how happy she'll be when we find Toni's murderer."

Luke glanced at Al. "Let's hope Jace can help with that. By the way, Rob still hasn't found out anything on Ethan's current whereabouts. He sold the marital home when his wife died and cleaned out the bank accounts. What Rob can't figure out is why he's come to a dead end when trying to establish what his new address is."

"Maybe he's couch surfin' with friends or he's been on the road and paid cash fer wherever he's stayin'," Al said. "But I'm sure Rob'll work it out. Now do me a favor, will ya'?" He swerved the car to a stop outside a truck stop diner. Reaching into his pocket, he handed Luke a handful of dollar bills.

"Mine's a chocolate shake and a waffle. Yers' is on me, but don't go crazy, ya' hear me?" He tapped the side of his nose and chuckled. "This is our little secret, Luke, got it? Cassie's on a healthy eatin' drive. She says Ima gettin' chunky. But you an' me both know catchin' killers is hungry work."

Luke grinned and grabbed the cash out of Al's hand. "It sure is, Boss. I'll be right back."

*****

"I guess this is what you kids would call a hipster kinda' place," Al said when they reached the address for the television studio facilities where Jace Carson worked. Conveniently located in the city, it was on the historical ship canal of North Lake Union in the heart of Seattle's Fremont neighborhood.

There were several studios nearby. They were surrounded by several of the world's largest software development companies, gourmet coffee houses, restaurants, boutique shops, and legendary music venues. He gawked at several people who were walking past them in the street. "Do ya' need a beard and tattoos to work around here, I wonder?"

"Just the guys," Luke said. He pointed at Al's chin. "You could lose the waffle syrup, though."

Al rubbed his chin with his finger and quickly stuck it in his mouth to remove the offending syrup. "Thanks," he mumbled. "I coulda' worked in the movies, ya' know, but my real life was more excitin'. Maybe someday they'll make a movie outta' the story of my life. Come to think of it, I should write a book about it and sell the screen rights. I was sorta' meanin' to do that when I retired, 'cept my retirement got delayed."

They walked into the lobby. "Who would you want to play you in the movie?" Luke asked casually.

Al looked serious. "It's a tough question. Ima thinkin' Al Pacino. He's not as good lookin' as me, although we do share a name. Or Ray Liotta, maybe? I liked him in Goodfellas."

Luke nodded back at him with a straight face. "Good choice. And do you have anyone lined up to play Cassie?"

"She might have somethin' to say about that. I'd have to let her decide."

The receptionist gave them directions to Jace's office, where they were met by a young man with a beard and wearing leather pants. "Mr. Carson won't be long," he said. "He's just finishing up an important call."

Al gave Luke a knowing glance, and they sat down to wait.

A man Al recognized from the photo on Toni's nightstand came out of his office several minutes later. Tall, with sandy hair, Al was pleased to note the stubble on his chin did not constitute a beard. It was more like a couple of day's growth.

"Jace Carson," the man said, offering a firm handshake to both Al and Luke, who introduced themselves in turn. "Please, come into my office, where we can speak in private. Can my assistant get you any refreshments? I don't know about you, but it's been a long day, and I haven't eaten. I could do with a beer and some snacks."

Al thought about the waffle and chocolate milkshake that were barely digested in his stomach, and the fajitas Cassie had said she was making for dinner. He shook his head. "Ima gonna' pass, Jace, thanks. But you two go ahead."

He watched as Young-Beardy-Guy-In-The-Tight-Pants entered

with beers for Jace and Luke within seconds of Jace buzzing through to him on the speakerphone, along with a tray of chips and dips and mini bowls of popcorn.

"Thanks fer agreein' to see us on such short notice," Al said, trying to ignore the urge to help himself to some of the chips. "We really appreciate ya' makin' time for us in yer' schedule. Especially under the circumstances. You have our heartfelt condolences, Mr. Carson."

"Please, call me Jace. I was expecting to hear from you, as Hillary told me when we spoke earlier that she'd hired you to take on the case." He looked directly at Al. "Unfortunately, I couldn't get out of being on set today, due to a diva presenter whose name I won't mention. It's essential that I'm around to deal with all of her quirky demands, otherwise we'd never wrap the show." He raked a hand through his hair. "I can't believe this is happening. Last time I saw Toni, I, we—" His voice cracked. "Sorry, I just need a few moments."

Observing someone's grief was always interesting for Al. There was a sense of voyeurism, of intruding on their privacy, but the insight it allowed into the person's character and whether their emotions were genuine was an invaluable part of judging whether they had anything to hide. In this case, he sensed Jace was trying to be strong and to hold himself together.

They sat in silence while Jace composed himself, the snacks on the table left untouched.

"I was about to say, the last time I saw Toni we shared a very special moment," Jace said, his eyes shining. "I proposed to her over dinner two nights ago. She was the love of my life. I didn't want to waste one second apart from her."

"What was her answer?" Al said, remembering the note beside Toni's bed. His eyes never left Jace's.

Jace gave him a sad smile. "I don't know. I guess I never will.

Toni was…hesitant about marriage. She'd had one bad experience of her own, and she felt her mother had been let down by her own husband in the last few years of her life. I told her to think it over and let me know when she got back from her vacation with Hillary. I think she probably wanted to run it past her sister. They were very close."

"Yeah," Al said. *I like this guy,* he thought to himself. *No airs or graces, no pretence. He says it like it is.*

"Jace, can ya' think of anyone Toni mighta' been havin' problems with?"

Jace took a swig of his beer. "I don't think it's a secret that Tyler Alexander had a grudge against her."

"Is that the blog guy?" Al said. "Munchies, or somethin'?"

"Nibbles," Luke corrected him.

"That's right," Jace went on. "They were involved in a legal dispute, and Toni wouldn't back down. As a result, Toni felt he was trying to ruin her business. She was aware Tyler had told several food magazines and other clients her work was substandard, and they should use her competitor, Food for the Soul Photography, instead. Thing is, Toni and the owner of that business got along great and actually recommended each other if one of them couldn't take a job. Her business was growing constantly, and Tyler didn't have much sway."

"What's your personal opinion of Tyler?" Luke asked. "Do you know him?"

Jace gave a wry smile. "Everyone knows him. He's an attention seeker. He lives large and documents pretty much everything on social media, although his online profiles have gotten rather quiet lately. He has a reputation for irrational behavior and is known to accuse others anytime something goes wrong. You'd need to speak with Toni's lawyer to get all the details, but Tyler pinned the blame on Toni for his blog earnings taking a nosedive recently. I wouldn't be surprised if he's overextended himself financially."

"I see," Al said. He observed Luke taking notes. "Did she ever mention anyone at work?"

Jace thought for a while. "Her assistant, Barrie, could be difficult, but Toni could handle it. She knew it came with the territory of being the boss. And there was that guy, the janitor, I think he asked her out a few times, but as far as I know there were no hard feelings when she told him it was never going to happen."

"Jes' to clarify, do ya' mean Hector Delgado?" Al wanted to be sure there was no misunderstanding, and that they were talking about the same person.

"That's the one," Jace said.

Somehow, Al hadn't pictured Hector as a mild-mannered janitor. But that was based on his knowledge about Hector's involvement with Hispanic militant groups, which Jace would not be aware of.

He glanced over to make sure Luke had documented everything before moving on. "What about her stepfather, Ethan Doyle, did Toni ever mention him?"

Jace shook his head. "Not really. I don't know much about Toni's family other than that her parents were dead, her mother had an unhappy second marriage, and Toni was very close to Hillary. She didn't like talking about her parents. I think it was upsetting for her, so I never pushed it. Toni introduced me to Hillary at a dinner at Canlis when Hillary was in Seattle a few months back. Do you know of it?"

"Yeah, I've met the Executive Chef, Gaspard Chastain," Al said, without going into details. He'd investigated the chef as part of a recent murder case when a woman was found dead at the Waterfront Palace development in downtown Seattle. "My wife likes the food there, but it's kinda' high cotton fer me, if ya' know what I mean.

Too many knives and forks to think about."

"That's a good point," Jace said, glancing at his watch. Looking back up at Al, his face was grave. "I'm really sorry. I have a meeting with the stars of the Good Lookin' Cookin' show regarding next week's segment, so I'm going to have to wrap this up. Believe me, dealing with some of the show presenters is hard work. I should know, I dated one once. Never again, is all I can say about that."

Al leaned in closer to Jace's desk. "Who was that? The reason I ask is because that's one of the lines of inquiry we're pursuing. It's possible a disgruntled ex of yers' mighta' been unhappy about ya' dating Toni and decided to do something about it."

"I don't have many exes," Jace said, "but the only one who might be crazy enough to do something like that is Sophia Waters, the presenter I was referring to. She's on 'Good Living in the Northwest'. It airs Monday mornings."

Young-Beardy-Guy-In-The-Tight-Pants put his head around the door and Jace looked up and shook his head. "Tell them I'll be a few more minutes, Chad. This is important."

Turning back to Al, he continued. "Sophia and I dated before I met Toni. We had fun, and it was a new relationship, but when I discovered she was making plans for us to move in together, I backed off and told her it was too soon. We dated for a little while longer, but it fizzled out. When I told her that it was over between us, she went off the deep end. It didn't stack up."

"Whaddya' mean?" Al said.

Jace sighed. "She said she was heartbroken and gave me a huge guilt trip. She sometimes engaged in the practice of self-harming. She'd intentionally cut her arm with a sharp knife. She claimed my calling off our relationship was another reason for her to cut herself. The thing is, apart from the obvious scars, I always allowed for the fact Sophia had psychological issues and was taking medication for them, because I'd seen several prescription bottles in her bathroom.

Because of that, I was always careful to go easy on her. But in the end, I had to make the break. She contacted me again recently, and I told her I still wasn't interested."

Al considered what Jace had told him. An unhinged ex-girlfriend bent on vengeance was a juicy lead in the case. "Do ya' know what kind of issues Sophia had, by any chance? Was there an underlyin' cause to the pattern of self-harm?"

"I looked at the prescription bottles one time," Jace said. "There was one for anxiety and another for depression. They were prescribed by her psychiatrist. I didn't think much about it because so many people are taking drugs for those problems these days. The staff in here are popping them like M&Ms."

Out of the corner of his eye, Al could see Luke writing a note.

Call Rob re shrink and Sophia's drugs.

Al stood up and Luke followed his lead. "Jace, this has been a great help. Thanks for yer' time and once again, condolences for yer' loss. We'll keep ya' informed of any developments."

"I'd appreciate it," Jace said, walking them to the door.

On the way out, Al counted four men with long groomed beards and tattoos. He drew a line at tattoos, far too painful in his opinion, but the other, he could do.

"Tell me Luke," he said as he strode down the hallway, "Ima considerin' jumpin' on the facial hair bandwagon. Seems like all them other sexy dudes already did." He pouted and stroked his chin with two fingers in a downward direction. "Whaddya think?"

The expression on Luke's face told him all he needed to know.

CHAPTER NINE

After the meeting with Jace and on the way to drop off Luke at his downtown Seattle apartment, Al called Rob using the Bluetooth speaker in his car.

"Rob, need ya' to get the skinny on Sophia Waters, an ex-girlfriend of Jace Carson's. She's got mental health issues and might just be unhinged enough to have done somethin' to Toni."

"Is that the television presenter?" Rob asked. "I've only seen her show a couple of times, but she comes across as nice. Easy on the eyes, too."

"That's the one," Al said. He recalled that Cassie had watched the show, and she had told him Sophia came off as a bubbly girl-next-door type who sometimes fluffed her lines when reading the teleprompter. She got away with it by fluttering her eyelashes and giggling a lot.

"Apparently, she didn't take it well when Jace broke up with her. See if ya' can speak to the shrink who prescribed her medication. Her doc may have some insight on whether she's capable of murder."

"Will do. I'm glad you called when you did," Rob went on, "because I just heard back from my source that the Hispanic militant group Hector belongs to is meeting in a couple of hours. Turns out

Hector hasn't attended in a while, but I've authorized my source to attend the meeting tonight and see what he can find out about him."

Al came to a stop outside Luke's apartment building, double-parked because there were no open curb spaces where he could park, and kept the engine running.

"What about Ethan Doyle?" Luke asked. "Any news on his whereabouts yet?"

They both heard Rob sigh. "He left Key West a while back, then the trail stops. He sold the house he lived in with his wife and seems to have disappeared into thin air. I'm starting to think Ethan Doyle might not be who he says he is."

"Did ya' check with all the agencies yer' not supposed to be able to get information from, but ya' always do?" Al asked with a chuckle.

"Yep," Rob confirmed. "The Department of Motor Vehicles and the airplane, bus, and train manifests all turned up nothing. I'm working on tracking his cell phone using GPS to try and get a trace on him that way.

"Call me if you need anything," Luke said, turning to Al and unfastening his seatbelt. "If not, see you both in the morning. Bye, Rob."

"Thanks, both of ya'," Al said, as Luke got out of the car. "Rob, Ima gonna end the call. Got one comin' through from Chief Hewson. Bye." The blast of a horn sounded from behind, and he muttered something under his breath and raised a hand in front of the driver's mirror as an apology for blocking the traffic lane.

"Yo, Chief," Al said, pulling away with a squeal of tires. "Whaddya' got?"

*****

"Smells good," Al said as he walked into the kitchen and over to where Cassie was standing by the stove beside a colorful array of fajitas sizzling on a skillet. He kissed her on her cheek. "Where's Hillary?"

Cassie smiled up at him. "She should be down in a moment. She was taking a nap and I went upstairs to wake her when you called to say you were just driving off the ferry. How did it go this afternoon?"

A bleary-eyed Hillary appeared and they both turned around. "Hi, Al." She yawned. "Did you see Jace?"

"I did," Al said, opening the refrigerator and taking out a chilled Mexican beer. "I'll tell you all about it over dinner."

Al brought them up to speed on the meeting with Jace, culminating in the news about Sophia Waters being a possible suspect. "I felt bad for Jace," he said, "the guy's clearly hurtin'. He was a pro about holdin' it all together, but I could tell how upset he was. The fact that he never got an answer from Toni on his marriage proposal almost choked me up. I wasn't sure whether to tell him about the note we found, so I kept quiet to be on the safe side." He reached for a tortilla and smothered it with guacamole and sour cream before heaping on the fajitas.

"What do you mean?" Cassie watched him try to roll the tortilla. Sauce dripped out one end as he lifted it to his mouth. "You always overfill it." She said as he took a big bite.

"I weren't sure it was my place to say anythin'," Al explained when he'd finished chewing. He wiped his chin with a napkin. "Also, I didn't know if tellin' him Toni's answer woulda' upset him more or been a comfort to him. Thought I'd leave it to Hillary to make the call on that one."

"Thanks, Al," Hillary said. "I have a feeling he'd like to know. I think it might bring him some relief. I'll speak to him about it, although I'd prefer to do it in person. I have a lot of time for Jace. We only met once, but from what I could tell, he adored Toni." She stared down at her plate and blinked away the tears from her eyes.

"It seems like the feeling was mutual," Cassie said. "It's so cruel the way Toni's life has been cut short, and Jace's has been ruined. If Sophia Waters is to blame, she's got a lot to answer for. They should lock her up and throw away the key."

"Let's not jump to any conclusions jes' yet." Al turned to Red, who was patrolling around the table in search of scraps and fed him a couple of pieces of meat. "We still have several other people we gotta' rule out first."

"I wish you wouldn't feed the dog at the dinner table," Cassie said with a frown.

"Red really has a soft mouth," Al said, still looking at Red. "Balto wouldn't be so dainty with treats like that. Balto's a friend's dog," he explained to Hillary with a sideways glance. "He's a bundle of fun. Not as wise or sensible as ol' Red here, but quite the character."

"That reminds me, Al, get ready for a surprise in the next few days," Cassie said with a wink.

"Aw, are DeeDee and Jake and Balto comin' to see the twins?" Al's face lit up.

"You'll have to wait and see. I can't say anything more. Just finish your dinner."

Al stared at his wife, and knew it was useless trying to coerce her into divulging any more information. He'd have to try and wheedle it out of her later.

"I spoke to Chief Hewson on the way home," he said. "They weren't able to pick up anythin' from the prints that were in the house or DNA. What he did say, though, is that the coroner has determined that Toni was shot by a .30 caliber bullet, probably from an antique gun called a Suicide Special. Them guns only took certain types of bullets. A police officer who's a ballistics expert was at the coroner's office on another matter and recognized it."

He explained the term referred to cheap guns that were commonplace in late 19th century America. Despite the fact that most cities did not allow the open carrying of weapons, almost everyone owned a gun, and many people carried them concealed. The average person couldn't necessarily afford a Remington, Colt, or Smith & Wesson, so there was a thriving market for low cost pistols.

"Thing about them was," Al went on, "they were poorly made of cheap metal and weren't particularly safe to shoot when they were made way back when, let alone today. They had no safety features at all. Many of the Suicide Specials that are still around aren't in very good condition. Even in the best of storage situations, some of 'em can deteriorate even without bein' handled. They're not the sorta' gun you wanna' be messin' with. It's also a bizarre choice of murder weapon, 'cuz it's more likely to be a collector's piece. Can't imagine who'd want to even own one."

Hillary was staring at him with wide eyes.

"Ain't much about guns I don't know, in case yer' wonderin'," he added.

Hillary started to speak. "My mother owned an antique gun. It had belonged to her great-grandfather, and Mom considered it to be a family heirloom. I remember she kept it locked up in a cabinet in the garage, because she didn't want Toni or me to have access to it when we were growing up."

Al straightened up in his seat. "Go on."

"She also had bullets for it, and she told us that's what made it so special, because the bullets were original to the gun. Kind of like the china soup tureen she'd inherited from her grandmother. She said it was very valuable because it had the original ladle in it."

Al thought for a few moments. "Do ya' know where the gun is, or what happened to it?"

"I haven't seen it for years," Hillary said. "When Mom married

Ethan, they moved from my parents' old house. Ethan said he didn't want to be living with my father's ghost. A lot of stuff went into storage."

"Did yer' mom have many valuable antiques like that, and what happened to 'em when she died?"

Hillary shrugged. "She didn't have many. Just a few. I can't say for sure what they were worth, because Ethan held an estate sale and sold everything after Mom died. The gun might have been in it. Come to think of it," she added, "he must have also sold the antique tureen, because I never saw that either. He pretty much cleaned out everything he could. I didn't go to the sale because it would have been too painful for me to see our mother's things being sold. Toni was living here on Bainbridge Island, so she wasn't at it either."

"Did Ethan give ya' any of the proceeds from the sale?" Al asked.

"Are you kidding?" Hillary gave an emphatic shake of her head. "Toni and I never got anything when our mother died. Ethan got rid of everything, even the jewelry that wasn't particularly valuable but had sentimental value to us." She stared off into space, pain etched across her face. "After that, he said he was going into seclusion for a while. I know he took that time to sell the house, because I had clients looking to buy who asked me to arrange for them to view the property, and I referred them to another agent. I know it sounds snarky, but I'm sure he sold her house, held the estate sale, cleaned out her bank accounts, and moved away."

Cassie spoke up. "When's the last time you saw him?"

"At the funeral," Hillary said, "so it's been a few months." She sniffed. "And I'm not in any hurry to ever see him again."

"Rob's been tryin' to find him and hasn't come up with anythin' yet," Al said. "He thinks he might be usin' a different name."

Hillary gasped. "Of course. I don't know why I didn't think of it before. At the wedding, Toni and I both signed the register as witnesses. I remember snickering when I found out that Ethan's first name is actually George. In fact, I asked him about it, and he said he's always been known as Ethan, even though it's not on his birth certificate."

Al eyed the remaining fajitas in the skillet Cassie had placed in the center of the table on a wooden board. "That explains a lot of things. If ya' ladies are done, Ima gonna' have one more tortilla and call Rob to let him know. Ethan's explanation sounds like a load of hooey, if ya' ask me."

"Go ahead, honey," Cassie said, and Hillary nodded. Cassie pushed the skillet towards Al.

"What else needs to be done tomorrow?" Hillary asked as she tried to stifle a yawn, not quite succeeding.

"Rob should have some info on Sophia's shrink," Al said between bites, "and he'll either call the shrink or set up an appointment with 'em. He's got someone getting' more info on Hector as well. I'd like to arrange to see Tyler Alexander if possible, and Ethan, or should I say George, Doyle is gonna' find out we're closin' in on him."

Cassie stood, and began to clear the dinner dishes.

"Let me help you," Hillary said, jumping up from the table.

"Absolutely not," Cassie said firmly. "You've got a busy day tomorrow, so you go on upstairs."

Hillary smiled at her gratefully. "Thanks. Good night, you two."

"Nite," Al and Cassie said in unison, as Hillary went upstairs. A few seconds later, Red followed her up.

"Now then," Al said, picking up his plate and taking it over to the dishwasher. "What was that you were sayin' about a surprise?"

Cassie smiled to herself and didn't respond.

CHAPTER SIXTEEN

Early the following morning, Al came downstairs to an empty kitchen. The patio doors were wide open, and Red wasn't around. A quick glance at the garden confirmed Red had most likely gone on an early walk with Hillary, the same as the previous day.

By the time Cassie joined him a while later, Al had brewed a pot of coffee and was on his second bowl of cereal. Cassie moved the cereal box off the table. She frowned, staring at the box like it was an alien object, and squinted at the list of ingredients.

"I certainly don't remember buying these chocolate-covered sugar bites disguised as a busy mom's alternative to a healthy breakfast," she said. "Are they even legal? There are so many additives, I'm not sure whether they should be classified as food or rocket fuel."

"Found 'em in the pantry," Al said with a shrug. "Briana musta' brought 'em over." Cassie's daughter Briana lived in Seattle but was a regular visitor to their home, and even more so since she'd started dating Luke several months earlier. An interior designer, she was looking for a fixer-upper property on Bainbridge Island she could renovate and often met Luke when he was finished working so he could look at properties with her. She'd even confessed to knocking on people's doors, unsolicited, to ask them if they'd be interested in selling their home. To date, that tactic had resulted in several polite refusals and several not-so-polite doors closed in her face. Al liked her go-getter attitude. "Keep slingin' yer hook' in the water til ya' getta' bite," he was fond of telling her, or words to that effect.

Cassie poured some coffee. "I'll have to speak to Briana about her nutrition. Ever since I started writing the Food Spy column, I've become a lot more aware of what we put in our bodies. I was thinking of starting a vegetable garden. That fresh tomato salad we had with the fajitas last night made me want to grow our own. What do you think?"

"I think it's a great idea," Al said, glancing outside. "If we dig up the ground along the boundary, it might stop Dino from taking a short-cut from next door through the shrubbery instead of using the driveway. He keeps creepin' up on me when I'm down on the dock and nearly gives me a heart attack."

"I think the Choco Breakfast Bites are more likely to give you a heart attack than Dino," Cassie said. "I'll ask Briana not to put temptation in your way like that. She's coming over for dinner tonight, so I'll have a word with her."

"If ya' insist," Al said. His phone buzzed, and he glanced down at the screen. "Yo, Rob," he said, accepting the call. "Any news?" He smiled at Cassie, who got up and began to make toast.

"Yes, I've heard from my source about Hector Delgado," Rob began. "Not only did Hector make an appearance at the Hispanic Group's meeting last night, he made a rousing speech about the importance of not diluting the Hispanic heritage. What's surprising is, he rarely attended any meetings before, and he certainly was never vocal at any of them. Seems like his attitude has taken a sudden about-face."

"What did he say in this impassioned speech of his?" Al asked. Cassie set some buttered toast in front of him, along with a pot of their friend DeeDee's homemade blackberry jam. He began to slather the jam onto the toast.

"It was all about how he realized the error of his ways dating white women in the past. He said he'd been guilty of having his head turned by many a pretty face regardless of color, but when it came to settling down and starting a family he advised the people at the meeting to be more discerning."

"Hmm." Al munched on his toast. "Hector thinks it's okay to date any woman, but his racism kicks in when it comes to marriage and kids, is that right?"

"Pretty much. He was encouraging the men to only marry Hispanic women, or their children would be mixed-race, lacking identity and spurned by both the white and Hispanic communities. He said an integrated society is a myth, and Hispanics need to stand up for themselves and not be duped into accepting the lie that multicultural families can live in harmony. In his opinion," Rob went on, "it can only lead to further Hispanic marginalization. He pointed the finger at the assembled group, saying they needed to take action without delay and spread the word, or face the consequences."

"Wow. Sounds like he really thought it through. I wonder what happened to make him change his mind." From what Al had learned from Toni's cell phone history, Hector had made numerous calls to Toni in the weeks before her death, including one on the day she died. "The guy was relentless in his pursuit of Toni to the point of stalkin' her. In fact, I'm surprised Toni never reported him to the authorities."

"Toni never reported who to the authorities?" Hillary had just walked into the kitchen with Red, and Al looked up.

"Hector Delgado," he mouthed to her. She rolled her eyes and turned to Cassie, who was pouring her a mug of coffee. Al stepped outside onto the patio to continue the call.

"Maybe somethin' happened to give him an epiphany," Rob said, as Al looked across the garden to where Cassie was thinking of digging her vegetable garden. Or rather, where he would most likely be doing the digging. "I've had an epiphany myself," he mumbled, his face lighting up. He congratulated himself inwardly on his idea.

I'll talk to Dino later, see if he wants to spring for half the cost of a gate between our gardens down by the water. I'll put a bell on the gate then I can hear him comin.'

"What was that?" Rob sounded confused.

Al chuckled. "Nothin', don't mind me."

"Here's the clincher," Rob said. "The evening Toni was murdered, Hector was in Portland. When Hector's speech was finished last night, another man stood up. He talked about how he had met with Hector the previous afternoon and driven him to Portland to speak to a group of men who are starting a chapter down there. Said he and Hector had talked to the men and gotten back very late that night, but it was worth it. Then he asked for referrals for recruits for the new chapter."

"How convenient," Al said. "Have ya' verified he was in Portland and his speech wasn't just an elaborate cover with some accomplice who was primed to say that?"

He listened while Rob explained how his guy had been in touch with a contact of his in Portland who did the same thing Rob's contact did for PI's and the police, infiltrating Hispanic groups. The two of them shared info, so Rob's guy called him to see if he could get confirmation that Hector was in Portland. "He was definitely there," Rob confirmed. "Plenty of people saw him."

"Guess we can eliminate him as a suspect, in that case," Al said. "What about Ethan? Any more progress now that ya' know his real first name is George?"

"Actually, it's George Henry Edward Doyle, to be precise. And yes, suddenly everything's fallen into place. He's in Seattle and has been for several weeks. He's renting a place down at the Waterfront Palace. A dating profile in the name of Henry Doyle, with Ethan's picture on it, was recently posted on the Sugar Cougars website. He has himself down as a Porsche-loving internet entrepreneur, but in reality, his current mode of transport is a beat-up old green Chevy.

He's looking for love again."

"On the prowl, more like." Al wondered how many women Ethan had conned. "Hope he meets a cougar who's more predatory than he is. Do we know his whereabouts when Toni was killed?"

"I'm still waiting for a trace on his phone's GPS to pinpoint his exact location during the window of time when the murder took place. We know he called Toni earlier in the day, but he wasn't the only person of interest to do so. Tyler Alexander also called her, as well as Hector, although we can rule Hector out."

Hillary peered out from the kitchen to see if Al was free, and he squeezed his thumb and index finger together indicating he wouldn't be much longer.

"I also got the name of the shrink Sophia Waters has been seeing," Rob went on. "My source had to cut the conversation short unexpectedly, and they didn't say anything we don't already know, just that she suffers from depression and anxiety. Do you want to give the doc a call and see if you can find out anything?"

"Sure, send me the details." Al was aware of Hillary hovering by the doorway. "Thanks, Rob. I'll talk to ya' later. Bye."

He turned to Hillary, who was wearing a worried expression. "Al, I was wondering if you would mind coming to Toni's house with me this morning?" she asked him. "I want to pick up a few more things. Cassie said I could stay here as long as I want, and I don't really feel comfortable going back there by myself."

Al walked towards her, placing a hand on her shoulder. "I'd be happy to. Ima gonna' make a quick call first, and then we'll go. How does that sound?"

A look of relief crossed Hillary's face. "Wonderful, thanks. I'll go get ready."

Hillary went back inside through the kitchen, and Cassie appeared before Al could dial the number Rob had just sent him. "Are you finished with breakfast?"

He grinned. "Yeah, Ima full of rocket fuel, and good to go."

"That's good." Cassie smiled. "I'll stop by the hardware store later today and buy you a shovel, so you can dig your own you know what."

"That's why I love ya'," Al said, blowing her a kiss. "Yer' always lookin' out fer me."

He glanced back at his phone and punched in the number for Dr. Chin, Sophia Waters' psychiatrist. After introducing himself and explaining he'd been hired by the sister of a woman who was murdered to help solve the case, and with the full cooperation of the Bainbridge Police Department because they were understaffed, he cut straight to the chase.

"The thing is, Dr. Chin, I need more information regardin' one of yer' patients, Sophia Waters. It's critical to the murder case."

"I'm sorry, Mr. De Duco, I'm not at liberty to discuss any personal information pertaining to the patients I'm treating. I'm bound by patient confidentially both professionally and ethically." Dr. Chin's tone was snappy. "To be frank, I'm surprised you don't know that."

The reply was exactly what Al had expected, and his response rolled off his tongue. "I know that due to HIPAA conformity ya' can't divulge any information on her, but it's my understanding that if a patient is a danger to herself or someone else, yer' under an obligation to say so. That's what Ima askin' ya', Doc, if ya' believe Sophia poses a threat to herself or anyone else?"

He heard Dr. Chin take a sharp inhalation of breath. "Absolutely not. I've been seeing her for over a year. Never, in all that time, have I ever felt that her own, or anyone else's life was in danger. Sophia has some, how shall I put it, issues…that are being worked on.

Medication is helping them. If anything, her actions are a typical cry for help. That's really all I can say."

Al continued regardless. "Just wonderin' Doc, did she ever discuss Toni Adams or Jace Carson with you? Toni's the woman who was murdered. Jace, as ya' probably know, is Sophia's ex-boyfriend who recently dumped her. Were any of Sophia's issues to do with the fact that she was angry at Jace seein' Toni, by any chance?"

"I'm sorry, but I can't elaborate any further. I hope you understand."

"Yeah, I get it. Thanks, Doc."

Al ended the call and glanced at his watch. The day was young, and he'd just eliminated two more suspects. He strode into the kitchen, where Red had his nose stuck in his dog dish. "Let's go buddy," Al said, bending down to pet his silken coat, and waiting for Red to finish eating. "We got work to do."

When Red was done, they went into the hallway and he yelled upstairs to Hillary. "Y'all ready up there?"

"Coming now!" she yelled back.

Al smiled. After going to Toni's house with Hillary, he decided he'd head for Seattle. It was time to pay both Tyler Alexander and Ethan Doyle a surprise visit.

CHAPTER SEVENTEEN

Al turned his car into the driveway of Toni's home, and noticed that papers were sticking out of the mailbox at the end of the driveway. There was also a newspaper lying on the doormat next to the front door. As he pulled up in front of the garage, Hillary searched around in her purse for the door keys. Red poked his head between the two front seats and stared at Al.

"I know that look," Al said. He got out and opened the door for Red, attaching his leash. "Ima gonna' walk Red over to a tree before we go into the house," he said to Hillary, who had climbed out the other side of the car and was walking towards the house. "Won't be long."

Hillary stopped and turned around. Sensing her hesitation, Al added, "Why don'tcha wait a sec, and we'll come in with ya'? We'll be right there."

Hillary smiled and waved them away. "It's fine, I'm just being silly. I'll go on ahead and grab my stuff. I'll probably be back out by the time you finish with Red."

"Fine. Jes' promise me ya' won't go into the great room, got it?"

"Promise."

Al watched Hillary enter the house and then began to stroll down the driveway with Red, letting him off the leash when they came to a cluster of trees. While Red was doing his business, Al walked a short distance to the mailbox and reached inside to remove its contents. He nodded to an elderly woman approaching with a black labradoodle on a leash. "Mornin'. Nice day fer a walk."

The woman's pace quickened, and when she reached where Al was standing she came to a stop. "Stay, Batman," she said to the dog, before looking up at Al. "I heard the terrible news about Toni. She was a good neighbor, and a very nice person. It's quiet around here, and we all look out for each other. It's been a big shock to our community. I wish I could have done something. Are you a relative of hers? I wanted to pass on my condolences to her sister."

Al gave her a warm smile. Although etched with fine lines, the skin on the woman's face was soft and pale, and her light blue eyes displayed her concern.

"Jes' a friend of the family," he said. He motioned towards the house. "Hillary's inside, if ya' wanna' speak to her?"

The woman shook her head. "I would, but I'm taking Batman to his Pawsalates class."

Al scratched his head. He had no idea what the woman was talking about, but it sounded vaguely like something Cassie went to on Monday nights.

"Please, tell her you spoke to Blythe Duncan," the woman continued. "I'll try and catch her next time she's here."

"I will," Al said, noticing the woman looking down the street. She was frowning.

"There's that car again," she muttered.

Al followed her gaze.

She pointed at a car parked half a block down the street. "That old green one. I've never seen it before this week, and since then it's been here several times, usually parked in the same place. No one seems to know who owns it."

When Al saw the battered Chevrolet, his heart began to thump. "Blythe, I gotta' go," he said, turning and breaking into a run back up the driveway. "Red!" he called, and the dog came bounding out from the trees and raced ahead, reaching the house several seconds before him. Red waited while Al caught up.

"Ssh," Al said, as they walked inside together. Red's ears pricked up as the hackles running down the center of his back stood up and turned a dark color. Al sensed that the dog knew something was wrong. He stopped and listened to where the sound of voices was audible from further down the hallway. Creeping slowly forward so the hardwood floor didn't creak, he inched towards the open doorway of the small office situated in the room next to the kitchen. Red by his side, he stopped to just where he could see into the room. Sizing up the situation, Al pulled his gun from his waistband, aimed, and got ready for the right moment to fire.

*****

When Hillary stepped inside Toni's house, the loss that had seemed more distant when she was at Al and Cassie's home immediately came back to hit her with a thud. She tried not to look at the family photos in the hallway, knowing if she did she would crumple into a mess that she wasn't sure she would recover from. Even so, she could feel Toni's eyes looking at her from the walls, her smile frozen for eternity.

She closed her eyes for a second. The smell of the house was familiar, Toni's scent still lingering in the air. Hillary realized it was the silence that was disconcerting, since usually the home was filled with noise. If it wasn't coming from Toni's incessant chatter, it was from music playing or a television set, or sometimes any combination of all three.

Making her way upstairs, she entered Toni's bedroom, where she sat on the edge of the bed. The pillows were still propped up the way Toni had left them, the pink silk bedspread creased from when her sister had been lying there with her laptop on the day she died, as was her habit. Hillary picked up the photo of Toni and Jace, and remembered she needed to call Jace about the note they'd found containing Toni's answer to his marriage proposal. It was bittersweet news she'd have to deliver.

Hearing Al moving around downstairs was the reality check she needed to get on with what she was there to do. She walked from Toni's bedroom into the small guest room next door. She stuffed the rest of her clothes into a large shopping bag she'd brought with her and then went into the bathroom.

A loud crash from downstairs made her stop. She held her breath. Someone was walking around downstairs, talking to themselves, banging doors and slamming into things. It didn't sound like Al. One thing was for certain, they weren't very happy about something.

Leaving her bag, Hillary headed for the stairs, looking through the banister spindles to make sure there was no one in the hallway. She went down the stairs and had reached the bottom step when a voice stopped her in her tracks. She froze and waited for the person to come into view.

"Well, lookie who's here." Ethan appeared at the bottom of the staircase and sneered at her, gun drawn. He took a step towards her, grabbed her by the hair, and said, "Don't just stand there, come on down." With that he yanked her off the bottom stair step.

Hillary winced as he pushed her down the hallway into Toni's small office, the gun poking into the small of her back. Inside the room, the bookcase was overturned, its contents strewn across the floor. The desk drawers had been pulled out and ransacked. Ethan shoved her from behind. "Over there," he commanded, "Sit in that chair where I can see you, and don't move."

Trembling, Hillary walked to the corner of the room and sat in the small armchair he'd indicated, facing her captor. She was desperately trying to think of a way to escape, but an overriding feeling of nausea was making it more likely that she was about to throw up. She half-retched, and took a gulp of air, urging herself to try and hold it together until Al got there.

Ethan's eyes glinted at her. "Sorry to have to do the same thing to you that I did to your sister, but now that you've seen the gun, you know too much, huh?" He smirked. "That's a shame for you, babe. Bad timing, is all. It might have been better for you if you hadn't come here today. At least you would have lived."

Hillary recognized the pistol he was holding as her mother's antique gun. She found her voice and asked, "What are you doing here, Ethan? I thought criminals never returned to the scene of the crime."

"The second time is easier, especially when you know a back way to get into the house unseen. I'm just looking for a couple of letters I sent your sister. When she told me she never wanted me to contact her again, I asked her to return the letters to me. I was embarrassed at having sent them. She told me I couldn't have them, that she'd put them somewhere safe."

"Is that why you killed her?" Hillary was incredulous.

"No, don't be ridiculous." Ethan smiled. "Her high spirits and feistiness were two of the things I loved about Toni. She was quite something." His face clouded over. "Shame how it happened, really. But it was her own fault."

"Why was that?" Hillary tried to look behind Ethan to see if there was any sign of Al, but from where she was sitting, her view into the hallway was obscured.

"She wouldn't see me." He shrugged and looked away for a moment before staring back at Hillary. "You see, I wanted to marry her, but she wouldn't give me the time of day. How could I have a chance to show her my charms when she wouldn't even talk to me? I gave her plenty of chances. Eventually, I'd had enough, and something inside me just snapped."

"Marry her?" Hillary's voice was a whisper.

"Yeah, why not?" Ethan took a step closer to Hillary, the gun pointed at her head. "I knew your mother had given one-quarter of your father's life insurance policy to her. I could have used that money." He chuckled. "Since she wouldn't see me, I decided I'd marry you when we both got back to Key West and get the money that way. I was pretty sure you'd be the sole beneficiary of Toni's estate."

It was Hillary's turn to laugh. "It's just as well you're about to kill me, Ethan, because I'd never marry you in a million years."

Ethan gave her a wounded stare. "I know I wasn't one of your favorites, but I figured in time you'd come around, just like your mother did. Too bad it won't happen, but there are other women out there I can meet on the dating sites, and who knows, maybe I'll get lucky and they'll have a couple of daughters."

"You're never going to get away with this, Ethan." *Come on Al,* Hillary was thinking to herself, *where are you? Please, hurry up.*

"Really? I think I already did." He pointed at her watch, a Tag Heuer encrusted with diamonds around the dial. When he spoke again, the volume of his voice was raised by several notches. "One good thing about the murder was that I was able to get a couple of nice pieces of jewelry your sister was wearing. That will help my financial position. I see you've got good taste in arm candy as well. At least your visit here will be worthwhile to me. Hand it over."

Hillary unclipped the clasp on her watch and removed it from her wrist. Wordlessly, she handed it to Ethan. His pupils were dilated, and a crazed look had come over him. Hillary had no idea if he was a drug user, but by the way he was acting, she wouldn't have been surprised.

She tried to look past Ethan again, and with a sinking feeling, realized her fate was sealed. Even if Al was in the house already and listening, which was probable, there was no way he could save her. Ethan was standing between her and the only escape route, the doorway. If she tried anything, Ethan would shoot her. If Al tried anything, Ethan would shoot her.

Either way, it looks like I'm going to get shot. Weighing her options, Hillary decided she had nothing to lose. *My only chance is to roll off this chair and hope Al can do something to Ethan before he kills me. If that doesn't work, I'm dead.*

In a split second she dove off the chair and scrambled towards Ethan's legs. At the same time, a shot rang out, and Ethan's gun flew out of his hand and landed across the room. Red leaped towards them and knocked Ethan to the ground beside Hillary. Ethan yelled in pain. "You son-of-a…you shot my hand," he moaned.

Hillary tried to jump to her feet to get away from Ethan, who was grabbing at her with his good hand, but she was having trouble getting to her feet. Her head still ached from where he'd pulled out a clump of her hair.

"Stay where ya' are or Red's gonna kill ya'," Al growled to Ethan, reaching over for Hillary's hand and helping her up. "Go outside and call the cops," he said to her, handing her his phone.

After Hillary left the room, Al picked up the antique pistol Ethan was going to use to kill Hillary and dropped it in his pocket. He kept his gun trained on Ethan who was still lying on the floor and said, "Ima thinkin' Ima jes' gonna' shoot and kill ya' right here and now."

"That's the way these kinda' situations always ended when I was with the Mob. Doin' that would save Hillary and others all the hurt of havin' to testify in court about yer' worthless self. Save the taxpayers the cost of puttin' on a big trial jes' to send ya' off to the slammer forever. I'll jes' tell the cops we had a little shootin' action and ya' lost, sucker. So get ready to meet yer maker."

Al levelled his gun at Ethan's head and cocked the hammer, but just as he did so he heard the sound of approaching sirens, and he realized it was too late for him to shoot Ethan, since the police would be arriving momentarily. He lowered his gun ad said, "Well, ain't this yer' lucky day. Guess ya' ain't gonna' have to try and lie yer' way through them purly' gates today after all."

Moments later the house was teeming with almost all the law enforcement personnel Bainbridge Island had to offer. For the second time in several days, Al and Hillary were questioned at length about the events at the house, and Al's stomach was rumbling by the time they were finally told they could leave.

A crowd had gathered at the end of the driveway, and as the police drove away with a handcuffed Ethan Doyle in the back seat, Al saw the woman he had been speaking to earlier, Blythe Duncan, approach Hillary. They spoke for a few moments, and he was glad that Blythe had been able to express her condolences to Hillary in person.

He pulled his phone out of his pocket and called home to update Cassie. "Let's celebrate," he said, after she'd congratulated him on catching another murderer and hopefully sending Ethan to prison for a long time. "Red was the star of the show. He ain't never done nothin' like that before, no trainin' at all. What a dog."

"He must be a natural, just like you," Cassie suggested.

"Yeah. What's fer lunch? I can pick up somethin' special."

"I've got it covered. I'll just change dinner to lunch," Cassie said. "I was going to marinate some fish and have some red potatoes with it. I'll add some garlic bread and a green salad with a chilled rosé and it will be lovely on the patio. Briana's already here, so why don't you invite Luke and Rob as well, and as a reward for Red, I'll defrost a steak for him."

"Perfect, I'll call the guys now. Oh, and Cassie?"

"Yes, Al?"

"What's, um, Pawsalates?"

Cassie laughed. "You've got to keep up with things, honey. It's pilates, you know for dogs."

CHAPTER EIGHTEEN

When they arrived back at the house, Cassie greeted Hillary with a warm hug before raising herself on tiptoe to kiss Al. "Well done, both of you," she said, steering Hillary through the kitchen doors and out onto the patio. Al and Red followed them outside. "That must have been a traumatic experience for you, Hillary."

Hillary nodded. "I think I'm still a little dazed. It was weird being held at gunpoint by the man who'd killed my sister. I knew Ethan was ready to pull the trigger on me as well. He had murder in his eyes." She smiled at Briana, who was setting the table. "Hi, I'm Hillary. You must be Cassie's daughter?"

Briana beamed at her. "That's me. Briana." She extended her hand to Hillary. "It's so nice to meet you, Hillary, despite the sad circumstances. I've heard all about you from my mom and Luke. You've been through a terrible time. I'm really sorry about what happened to your sister."

Red, his head held high and trotted over to stand next to Hillary. She petted him before replying, and he promptly flopped onto the patio tile floor at her feet. "Thanks, Briana. It's been tough, but after what happened this morning I feel like I can put the worst behind me. I'm lucky to be alive, which is a life-changing feeling. I guess it puts everything into perspective. Your mom and Al have been amazing, and Red's been my rock."

Briana lifted a bottle of chilled rosé from the wine bucket sitting in the center of the table. "In that case, can I tempt you with some wine?"

Hillary gave her a grateful smile. "Definitely."

Briana began to pour.

By the time Luke and Rob arrived, the three women and Al had already polished off a bottle of Provence's finest.

"Glad yer' here, guys," Al said, looking up. "I was outnumbered."

"Come and help me," Cassie said, pulling on Al's sleeve. "You're on wine duty. I'll serve lunch."

The meal turned into a leisurely afternoon of delicious food in laid-back surroundings, good wine, and friendly conversation. Enjoying the opportunity to play up to an audience, Al regaled them with his version of the showdown with Ethan, right down to rolling off his chair in an imitation of Hillary's diversion tactics that allowed Al the chance to shoot the gun out of Ethan's hand. He decided not to tell them about his aborted plan to simply shoot and kill Ethan. *Some things are better left unsaid*, he thought to himself.

"Ima tellin' ya'," Al said, sprawled out on the tile patio floor, "If Hillary hadn't taken that nosedive when she did, I'm not sure what woulda' happened. We might not be havin' this celebration lunch." It was a sobering moment.

Al climbed up onto his feet and dusted himself off, and Hillary spoke up. "Al, you were wonderful. For a moment I thought I was done for, but I knew if anyone could get me out of there alive it was you. For that, I will be eternally grateful." Her eyes welled up as she looked at Al, before turning to Cassie. "And Cassie, thank you for making me so welcome in your home and for everything you've done for me. I can never repay you."

"You don't have to," Cassie said, reaching out across the table to squeeze her hand. "That's what friends are for. You're always welcome here, please remember that."

Hillary nodded, and paused. "And I'm not forgetting Luke and Rob, of course. What you guys do is beyond awesome. You're the best." She looked across the table, smiling at both of them. "Last, but not least..."

Everyone followed her gaze to where Red's head was in his dog dish which was filled with tender chunks of steak lovingly cooked on the grill by Al.

"Red," she continued. "My hero."

Al cleared his throat. "Mine too."

"Mine three," Briana, said, and everyone laughed.

After lunch, the group lingered over a cheese board and crackers. "Have you decided what you're going to do next?" Cassie asked Hillary. "Please, know the invitation to stay here as long as you like still stands."

"Thanks, Cassie. I'd certainly like to stay for a few days to give me the chance to meet with Jace and finalize the funeral arrangements. There's Toni's house to think about, as well."

"Next time you go there, the great room will have been stripped and cleaned," Rob said. "I made the arrangements myself. The mess in the office will be dealt with too, so don't give that another thought. Are you planning on selling the house? It's a beautiful piece of property, and I'm sure it will get snapped up immediately."

"I might be interested," Briana said, nodding.

Hillary shook her head. "I'm not listing it for now. Toni loved that place, and I know why. It's like the vacation cottage we stayed in every summer with our parents when we were little. Right down to the narrow staircase leading to the attic rooms and the wildflowers growing by the water's edge. For Toni, that home evoked happy memories. I'm considering moving in myself."

"Really? What about your business back in Florida?" Cassie asked.

"I'm ready for a change from real estate," Hillary explained. "I'd already been thinking of alternative careers for a while before any of this happened. There's nothing keeping me in Florida now that my mother's not there. Toni had asked me if I'd be interested in joining her in her Food Porn Photography business, and I was considering it." She looked around the table. "Something in my gut is telling me to give it a try. I think Toni would approve."

"Ima thinkin' she would too," Al said. He made a sign of the cross and raised his eyes to the sky, while whispering under his breath. "I know a few people up there," he said to Hillary when he'd finished mumbling. "Jes' havin' a word, askin' them to look out fer Toni fer ya'." Cassie tenderly patted his arm, nodding her approval.

"I appreciate that, Al. Do you know any decorators, by any chance?" Hillary went on. "I'll have to get the house repainted and change some of the furniture. I know what I like, but I'm pretty clueless when it comes to doing anything like that myself."

Al's eyes settled on Briana, whose face flushed. He raised his eyebrows and chuckled. "Ain't like ya' to be shy, Briana."

Hillary frowned. "Have I missed something?"

"I'm an interior designer," Briana explained. "I'd be happy to show you my portfolio to give you an idea of what I can do. Special rates for friends, of course."

"I'd like that a lot," Hillary said, beaming. "And now, I'd like to propose a toast." She raised her glass. "To new beginnings."

They all clinked glasses. "New beginnings."

Red woofed.

EPILOGUE

"Them twins are somethin' special," Al said to Cassie as she stood by the kitchen stove. He handed her his phone. "Look at this picture of me with little Vinny and Em. Four weeks old, and they're smart as a whip. Runs in the family, I guess."

Cassie smiled at the screen. "You can tell that already? They're cute as a button, that's for sure. A little birdie told me Roz and Clark had something to ask you, did they say anything when you were there?"

Al gulped. He pulled a handkerchief out of his pocket, his eyes welling up. "You been speakin' to DeeDee?"

Cassie nodded, and grinned. "Don't go getting all emotional. Tell me what they said."

"Ima gonna' be the godfather to baby Vinny," Al said, raising the handkerchief to his eyes. "In the religious sense, not the other, if ya know whadda mean. Look at me, blubberin' like a wimp. Ima turnin' into an old softie."

Cassie opened her arms to him. "Come here. You'll always be my favorite softie, if that's any consolation." She wrapped him in a hug, her head only reaching to his chest.

A fluffy gray ball of fur raced across the kitchen floor and snapped at Al's heels. He looked down. "Ow. This ankle biter is another wise guy. He's just as smart as Balto and Red, ain't that right, Spike?"

Spike, a husky puppy with a black studded collar and eyes the color of coal, barked.

"That's a high bar to set," Cassie said.

Al lowered his voice. "I know. In fact, no disrespect to either Balto or Red, but this little fella might just beat 'em both in terms of doggie IQ." He leaned down and placed a kiss on Cassie's lips. "Best surprise ever, the day you brought Spike home for me."

Cassie smiled, and pulled away to stir the pan of sauce she had cooking on the stove. "That's because you thought the surprise was going to be a gym pass, or something healthy."

Al shrugged. "Another dog to walk and play with sounds pretty healthy to me. Ima glad Red and Spike get along. And they love it when Hillary comes over and takes them both down to the beach. She seems to like Bainbridge Island, don'tcha think?"

"She told me the best thing she ever did was to quit work and list her home in Key West. Ever since she came back from Florida, she's thrown herself into remodeling Toni's old place. Rob's been helping her find her way around the area and showing her the sights of Seattle. The two of them are coming over for dinner later, along with Briana and Luke, so we've got a full house. I got the recipes for tonight's dinner from DeeDee."

Al peered into the saucepan. "Can't say as I know what that is, but I'm sure it's good, if you've used this half-empty bottle of wine on the counter. Just as well I wasn't savin' it," he sniffed.

"It's for a good cause," Cassie chided him. "You know how we both love having the young people over. Briana and Luke seem to be getting serious, and I wouldn't be surprised if there's another budding romance in the offing between Hillary and Rob. Oh, and I forgot to tell you. When I was talking to Hillary earlier she told me she'd gone into Seattle and met with Jace. She gave him the piece of paper Toni had on her nightstand."

"Ya' mean the one where she says she's gonna' tell him yes?"

"That's the one," Cassie said. "She said it was one of the hardest things she'd ever done. He was so emotional he couldn't speak for a long time. She also said she was glad she'd done it, because she felt it gave him closure knowing that Toni was ready to commit to him, even if it couldn't be. She said she hoped he'd find someone else, and if she hadn't done that, it might have held him back from ever having another serious relationship."

"Hmph." Al gave an eye roll. "Feel like Ima runnin' a datin' agency sometimes, instead of a PI firm. So, jes' what is it you're cookin' up?"

"We're having a brie and raspberry appetizer washed down with champagne, seared duck breast with wine sauce, rice pilaf, and a butter leaf lettuce salad. For dessert, there's brownies with bacon bits."

"Honey," Al said, kissing her again, "it all sounds delicious. But in the future, ya' probably better go back to hamburgers and real men food, huh?"

"Why is that?"

Al pulled two wine glasses from the cabinet, lifted the half-empty bottle of wine that was sitting on the counter next to the stove and poured them each a glass. He handed one to Cassie. "Spike an' Red gonna' turn their noses up at all this fancy stuff like we're havin' tonight. Either that, or they'll be gettin' all uppity and expectin' it all the time."

Cassie sipped her wine. "I can arrange hamburgers for the dogs, no problem. By the way, I spoke to DeeDee about the trip you mentioned. You know, the one to the Cayman Islands. She's definitely interested She's going to ask Jake about possible dates and let me know."

"That's good. It'll be nice to spend some time with 'em. Got plenty of room at my place in the Caribbean for all of us. Ima lookin' forward to some downtime."

"Really?" Cassie raised an eyebrow. "I'm not sure you understand the meaning of the word. I know I can't wait to sample some of the local cuisine. Strictly off-duty, no reviews involved. I'll leave it to DeeDee to pick up a few recipes while we're there. She never switches off when it comes to food."

Al gazed into Cassie's eyes. "Sounds like a plan. No work on this trip. Just rest, relaxation, and plenty of sun and sailin'. Deal?"

"No murder investigations?"

"Definitely no murder investigations."

Cassie's face lit up. "Then, you have yourself a deal. I love you, Al De Duco." She snuggled closer to him.

Al put his arms around her and wondered at the twists and turns that had brought him to this point in his life. "And I, you, Mrs. De Duco. Ain't got no idea how I lucked out to find myself with such a wonderful wife and a joyful home. Ya' make me the happiest I've ever been. Thank you, sweetheart."

Spike rubbed against his ankles, and Red walked over to join them. Al chuckled. "Did I mention 'bout hangin' out with two of the best dogs in the world? It just keeps gettin' better."

RECIPES

THE ULTIMATE PATTY MELT FOR TWO

Ingredients:
1 tbsp. vegetable oil
2 cups yellow onion, cut in ¼" slices
1 tsp sugar
1 tsp. apple cider vinegar
1 tbsp. ketchup
1 tbsp. sweet relish
1/8 tsp. Worcestershire sauce
¼ cup mayonnaise
Dash of cayenne
8 oz. hamburger (85/15% fat)
2 tbsp. butter, melted
4 slices rye bread (corn, Jewish, dark, whatever you prefer)
4 slices American cheese
4 slices Swiss cheese

Directions:
In a medium sauté pan, heat the vegetable oil over medium-low heat. Add the onions, sugar, and apple cider vinegar. Cook the onion, stirring occasionally for 30 minutes, until the onions begin to look like jam.

While the onions are cooking, make the patty melt sauce. In a small bowl combine the mayonnaise, ketchup, relish, Worcestershire sauce, and cayenne. Cover and refrigerate until ready to use.

Divide the hamburger into two halves. Shape the burgers to fit the shape of the bread, sort of an oval or oblong shape. Cook them on the BBQ grill or in a frying pan for approximately 3 minutes each side, or to taste.

Assembly:
Assemble the first patty melt by spreading 1/4 of the melted butter on one side of the rye bread. Place the buttered side down on a cutting board and place 2 slices of American cheese on the unbuttered side (there may be some overlap.)

Place 1 of the burgers on top of the cheese, followed by half the sauce, half the onions, and 2 slices of Swiss cheese. Top the patty melt with a slice of rye bread and spread 1/4 of the melted butter on it. Repeat process for second patty melt.

Place the patty melts in a frying pan over medium-high heat. Using the flat side of a spatula, press them down. Cook about 1 minute, and then carefully flip them over, cooking another minute or until golden brown. Remove, cut in half and serve. Enjoy!

NOTE: Grilled peaches go great with these.

GRILLED PEACHES ON THE BBQ

Ingredients:
2 peaches (Ripened and just barely soft. Usually 2-3 days after purchased.)
4 tbsp. brown sugar
1 tsp. ground cinnamon
1 tbs. olive oil

Directions:
Cut peaches in half, lengthwise. Remove the pit. Spoon out the

red material and discard, leaving yellow flesh of peach with hollowed-out pocket. Do not remove skin. Mix brown sugar and cinnamon together in a small dish.

Brush a light coat of olive oil on the flesh side of peaches and place flesh side down on hot BBQ grill for 4 minutes. Using a large metal long handled kitchen spoon, gently turn the peaches over so the skin side is down. Cook 5 more minutes.

After peaches have been turned over, place 1 tablespoon of brown sugar mixture in the hollowed-out pocket of each peach half and continue cooking until mixture melts. Keep lid down on BBQ. Gently remove peaches with a large spoon, being very careful not to spill the melted mixture. Plate and enjoy!

NOTE: The melted mixture is very hot and will burn your mouth. Be careful!

SEARED DUCK BREAST W/CHERRY WINE SAUCE

Ingredients:
4 5-6 oz. skin on, duck breast halves (Available frozen at Whole Foods or order online from Marysduck.com)
2 tbsp. butter, divided
1 large shallot, peeled and finely chopped
¼ cup chicken stock
15 red cherries, pits removed, halved
4 tbsp. red wine
1 tbsp. honey
1 tsp. balsamic vinegar
4 tbsp. brown sugar (If you prefer a sweeter sauce, use more.)
1 tsp. fresh rosemary, finely chopped
2 tbsp. cherry preserves
3 cloves garlic, finely chopped
Cornstarch (1/4 tsp. if needed)
Salt and pepper to taste

Directions:

Sauce:
Start the sauce 20 minutes before you start cooking the duck. You can hold the sauce until the duck is cooked. In a small saucepan heat 1 tbsp. butter over medium heat and cook the chopped shallot until soft, about 4 minutes. Add the garlic and cook 1 minute. Add chicken stock, cherries, red wine, honey, balsamic vinegar, brown sugar, rosemary, and cherry preserves.

Bring to a gentle boil over medium high heat until the sauce is reduced by half and becomes glazed. Cut about half of the cherry halves in half with scissors. Add all of the cherries to the sauce. Stir often for 10 minutes, reducing heat as sauce thickens. If not thick enough, mix ¼ tsp. cornstarch with about 1 tbsp. water and slowly add mixture to sauce to thicken it. Remove from heat, add 2 tbsp. butter and swirl around until dissolved. Return to stovetop and turn heat to very low. Keep warm until ready to serve.

Duck:
Place duck breast halves between 2 sheets of plastic wrap. Pound lightly to even thickness (about ½ to ¾ inch). Discard plastic wrap. Using a sharp knife with a thin blade, score skin in ¾" wide diamond pattern (don't cut into the flesh) by making 4 – 5 passes in each direction. The knife forms the diamond pattern. This can be done up to 8 hours before cooking. If doing ahead keep in refrigerator until 1 hour before cooking.

Melt 1 tbsp. butter in a heavy large skillet over medium-high heat. Lightly salt and pepper duck. Add duck, skin side down, to skillet and cook until skin is browned and crisp, about 5 minutes. Turn duck breasts over and reduce heat to medium. Cook until browned and to desired doneness, about 4 minutes longer for small breasts and 8 minutes for larger breasts for medium-rare. Remove from skillet, tent with foil, and let rest 5 minutes. (If you slice the duck too early, the juice will run out.)

Thinly slice duck. Fan slices out on plates. Spoon sauce over the slices and serve. Enjoy!

JULIE'S CHOCOLATE CHIP COOKIES

Ingredients:
½ cup rolled oats, regular or quick
2 ¼ cups all-purpose flour
1 ½ tsp. baking soda
½ tsp. salt
¼ tsp. cinnamon
1 cup butter, room temperature
¾ cup brown sugar, firmly packed
¾ cup granulated sugar
2 tsp. vanilla extract
1 tsp. lemon juice
2 eggs
3 cups semisweet chocolate chips
Parchment paper
Optional: 1 ½ cups chopped walnuts

Directions:
Preheat oven to 350 degrees. Cover 2 cookie sheets with parchment paper. Place the rolled oats in a food processor or blender and process until finely ground. Combine oats, flour, baking soda, salt, and cinnamon in a mixing bowl.

In another bowl cream the butter, sugars, vanilla, and lemon juice together using an electric mixer. Add eggs and beat until fluffy. Stir the flour mixture into the egg mixture, blending well. Add the chocolate chips and nuts, if desired, and mix well. Make balls with about ¼ cup of dough for each cookie and place 2 ½ inches apart on the prepared cookie sheet. Bake until cookies are lightly browned, 16 – 18 minutes. Transfer to a wire rack to cool completely. Enjoy!

ULTIMATE TOMATO SALAD

Ingredients:
10 leaves of lettuce
2 ripe tomatoes, chilled in refrigerator a few hours before serving

5 slices bacon, fried crisp and crumbled
2 tbsp. blue cheese
Blue cheese dressing (I like Bob's Big Boy.)

Directions:

Divide the lettuce and place on two salad plates. Slice the tomatoes, discarding the ends. Arrange the tomatoes on the lettuce. Spoon desired amount of dressing on the tomatoes. Scatter bacon and blue cheese on top. Enjoy!

SURPRISE!

PUBLISHING 9/22/18
MURDERED BY NEWS

BOOK FOUR OF
THE MIDWEST COZY MYSTERY SERIES

http://getBook.at/News

He was a Pulitzer Prize winning publisher. She was a celebrity newscaster. Someone hated one of them enough to commit murder.

Over 450,000 books have been sold by this two-time USA Today Bestselling Author. You can read all of them for free with Kindle Unlimited.

Kat's shocked when she's asked to help solve the murder but looks like her daughter may be marrying into the decedent's family. Sometimes you just have to do the right thing. Nice to know there's a Rottweiler at your back!

Open your smartphone, point and shoot at the QR code below. You will be taken to Amazon where you can pre-order 'Murdered by News'.

(Download the QR code app onto your smartphone from the iTunes or Google Play store in order to read the QR code below.)

ABOUT THE AUTHOR

Dianne lives in Huntington Beach, California, with her husband, Tom, a former California State Senator, and her boxer dog, Kelly. Her passions are cooking, reading, and dogs, so whenever she has a little free time, you can either find her in the kitchen, playing with Kelly in the back yard, or curled up with the latest book she's reading.

Her award winning books include:

Cedar Bay Cozy Mystery Series
Kelly's Koffee Shop, Murder at Jade Cove, White Cloud Retreat, Marriage and Murder, Murder in the Pearl District, Murder in Calico Gold, Murder at the Cooking School, Murder in Cuba, Trouble at the Kennel, Murder on the East Coast, Trouble at the Animal Shelter, Murder & The Movie Star, Murdered by Wine, Murder at the Gearhart

Cedar Bay Cozy Mystery Series - Boxed Set
Cedar Bay Cozy Mysteries 1 (Books 1 to 3)
Cedar Bay Cozy Mysteries 2 (Books 4 to 6)
Cedar Bay Cozy Mysteries 3 (Books 7 to 10)
Cedar Bay Cozy Mysteries 4 (Books 11 to 13)
Cedar Bay Super Series 1 (Books 1 to 6)... good deal
Cedar Bay Super Series 2 (Books 7 to 12)... good deal
Cedar Bay Uber Series (Books 1 to 9)... great deal

Liz Lucas Cozy Mystery Series
Murder in Cottage #6, Murder & Brandy Boy, The Death Card, Murder at The Bed & Breakfast, The Blue Butterfly, Murder at the Big T Lodge, Murder in Calistoga, Murder in San Francisco, Murdered by Superstition

Liz Lucas Cozy Mystery Series - Boxed Set
Liz Lucas Cozy Mysteries 1 (Books 1 to 3)
Liz Lucas Cozy Mysteries 2 (Books 4 to 6)
Liz Lucas Super Series (Books 1 to 6)... good deal

High Desert Cozy Mystery Series
Murder & The Monkey Band, Murder & The Secret Cave, Murdered by Country Music, Murder at the Polo Club, Murdered by Plastic Surgery, Murder & Mega Millions

High Desert Cozy Mystery Series - Boxed Set
High Desert Cozy Mysteries 1 (Books 1 to 3)

Northwest Cozy Mystery Series
Murder on Bainbridge Island, Murder in Whistler, Murder in Seattle, Murder after Midnight, Murder at Le Bijou Bistro, Murder at The Gallery, Murder at the Waterfront, Murder and Food Porn

Northwest Cozy Mystery Series - Boxed Set
Northwest Cozy Mysteries 1 (Books 1 to 3)
Northwest Super Series (Books 1 to 6)

Midwest Cozy Mystery Series
Murdered by Words, Murder at the Clinic, Murdered at The Courthouse, The Professor's Predicament

Midwest Cozy Mystery Series - Boxed Set
Midwest Cozy Mysteries 1 (Books 1 to 3)

Jack Trout Cozy Mystery Series
Murdered in Argentina

Coyote Series
Blue Coyote Motel, Coyote in Provence, Cornered Coyote

Midlife Journey Series
Alexis

Red Zero Series
Red Zero 1, Red Zero 2, Red Zero 3

Newsletter
If you would like to be notified of her latest releases please go to www.dianneharman.com and sign up for her newsletter.
Website: www.dianneharman.com,
Blog: www.dianneharman.com/blog
Email: dianne@dianneharman.com

Made in the USA
Middletown, DE
27 September 2018